ACCORDING TO JENNINGS
ESPECIALLY JENNINGS!
JENNINGS AND DARBISHIRE
JENNINGS ABOUNDING
JENNINGS AGAIN!
JENNINGS AS USUAL
JENNINGS AT LARGE
JENNINGS FOLLOWS A CLUE
JENNINGS IN PARTICULAR
JENNINGS, OF COURSE!
THE JENNINGS REPORT
JENNINGS' DIARY
JENNINGS' LITTLE HUT
JUST LIKE JENNINGS
LEAVE IT TO JENNINGS
OUR FRIEND JENNINGS
SPEAKING OF JENNINGS
TAKE JENNINGS, FOR INSTANCE
THANKS TO JENNINGS
THAT'S JENNINGS
THE TROUBLE WITH JENNINGS
TRUST JENNINGS!
TYPICALLY JENNINGS

Jennings Goes to School

Anthony Buckeridge

HOUSE OF STRATUS

This edition published in 2008 by House of Stratus, an imprint of
Stratus Books Ltd, 21 Beeching Park, Kelly Bray,
Cornwall, PL17 8QS, UK.

www.houseofstratus.com

Printed and bound by CPI Group (UK) Ltd, Croydon, CR0 4YY

A catalogue record for this book is available from the British Library
and The Library of Congress.

ISBN 0-7551-0159-6

Contents

Foreword

Jennings first made his appearance as a new boy in the London Children's Hour in the autumn of 1948. He and his friend Darbishire were then very new boys indeed. Mr Carter and the Headmaster, the very old Old Boy and the very Very Important Parent, were only names; Mr Wilkins' geometry lessons and Matron's cakes were joys still to come. We had not yet been thrilled by the adventure of the Poisonous Spider, or delighted by the Ingenious Affair of Jennings and the Tinkling Glass, or stirred to laughter by the antics of Leading Fireman Cuppling. All these characters have since delighted many thousands of Children's Hour listeners. Jennings has three times reached the distinction of an appearance in Children's Hour Request Week. On two of these occasions the plays came third with one in every two children voting for them. I hope that as many of them as have found their way into this story version of Jennings' adventures will prove as acceptable in print as they certainly have over the air.

DAVID DAVIS,
Producer, BBC Children's Hour.

Introduction

It would be a waste of time to describe Linbury Court Preparatory School in great detail, because, if you are going to follow Jennings through his school career, you will be certain to alter the shape of the building so that it becomes, in imagination, your own school. Jennings' classroom will be your classroom; his desk, your desk; his text books – well, those who want to know where Jennings was at school, have only to glance at his text books to find out. If you will open his *A Shorter Latin Primer*, carefully altered to read *A Shorter Way of Eating Prime Beef* you will find the inscription:

"If this book should dare to roam,
Box its ears and send it home,
to J C T Jennings,
Linbury Court School,
Dunhambury,
Sussex,
England,
Europe,
Eastern Hemisphere,
Earth,
near Moon,
Solar System,
Space,
near More Space."

This should satisfy the most inquisitive. But our search for geographical detail has led us too far ahead. Jennings has not yet arrived at Linbury; the Latin Primer is still unsullied, and JCT Jennnings is only a name on Mr Carter's list of new boys. So let's start at the beginning.

1

Jennings Learns the Ropes

It was the first afternoon of the Christmas term and Mr Carter was enjoying the peace and stillness, so soon to be shattered by the arrival of sixty-seven boys on the school train. A few had already arrived by car, and were importantly memorising the contents of the notice board in order to be first with the news when the main body arrived. To know who was who in such matters as prefects, dormitory captains and school librarians was important in itself, but to be able to broadcast this information to the masses before anyone else could get a word in edgeways, was more important still.

Mr Carter was greeted enthusiastically by the group at the notice board.

"Oh, sir, how are you, sir? Have you had a decent holiday, sir?" came from ten voices simultaneously.

"We had a supersonic time, sir," said an eleventh voice. "We went to Scotland, sir, and we had gluey porridge every day and we got stuck in a bog, sir, and my father said that was where they got the porridge from, but it was only a joke really, sir."

The twelfth voice added its quota.

"Sir, we went to France, sir, and we had a spivish ozard crossing, but I wasn't sea-sick, honestly, sir. It's a jolly wizard

1

job I'm not a chap I know at home's uncle, because he's always ill on boats, isn't it, sir?"

"Isn't it what?" said Mr Carter.

"Isn't it a good job I'm not him, sir."

"Who?" asked Mr Carter.

"The chap I know at home's uncle, sir."

"Yes, very probably," replied Mr Carter.

Twelve times Mr Carter shook hands; twelve times he was pleased to say that his health was excellent, and twelve times he informed the earnest inquirer that he had spent a pleasant holiday. He moved on, his right hand somewhat stickier than before.

In the dining-hall, where he stopped to pin up the plan of the boys' places at table, the Headmaster was showing a clergyman round the school. The latter, whose look of anxious inquiry clearly labelled him "New Parent," was accompanied by a small-scale model of himself, labelled with equal clarity, "New Boy."

The likeness between father and son was remarkable; both had fair, curly hair, Father's being thinner on top, but tidier; both had pale-blue eyes and spectacles and, when they spoke, both the large and the small edition expressed themselves in a welter of glistening consonants, and managed to convey the impression that they were speaking in capital letters.

"Now one attractive feature of this dining-hall, Mr Darbishire," the Headmaster was saying, "is that the air is kept at an even temperature by heated panels let into the walls."

"Really! Most interesting, most interesting!" said Mr Darbishire, in block capitals.

"And these windows are all fitted with vita glass, which means that they allow the ultra-violet rays to pass through."

The Reverend Percival Darbishire peered closely at the

vita glass windows, screwing up his eyes as though uncertain of the effect that the ultra-violet rays might be having upon his eyesight. It looked like ordinary glass to him, but one could never tell, and he was determined to be impressed by all he saw.

"Most remarkable, most remarkable!" he said.

"You will observe our system of overhead ventilation," the Headmaster went on, "which allows every boy a minimum of three thousand, five hundred cubic yards of air."

Mr Darbishire, still blinded by science, was unable to see anything overhead, except the electric light fittings, but he obediently looked upwards, wondering vaguely whether a tea-urn at the far end of the hall might have something to do with the ventilation.

"Most interesting! Very remarkable and – ah – interesting," he said, now convinced that the tea urn must have something to do with it.

The Headmaster was wondering whether he really did mean three thousand, five hundred cubic yards of air. Perhaps it was three hundred and fifty thousand cubic feet. He would have to work it out. There were twenty-seven cubic feet in a cubic yard, so that meant... He gave it up; after all, you couldn't expect a classical scholar to be a genius at mathematics as well.

"Good gracious, it's four o'clock!" he said, changing the subject. "Now you must come along to my study for a cup of tea."

Mr Carter returned to his room just as the patter of little feet announced that the main body had arrived by the school train. The little feet pattered up the stairs like a cavalry regiment thundering across the plain, and Mr Carter was once more the centre of vociferous greeting.

"Have you had a wizard holiday, sir?"

"Yes, thank you, Temple."

3

"So did we, sir," said Temple. "We went to Guernsey by air; it was super-delectable. Actually it was a rotten swizzle, sir, because we flew through low cloud and we couldn't see a thing, but if it hadn't been for that, and if we'd flown about a hundred miles farther east, I could have wiped this school right off the map, sir, honestly."

"Really!" marvelled Mr Carter.

"If I'd had a machine gun that is," Temple explained.

"We seem to have had a narrow escape."

Mr Carter turned to the next boy.

"Well, Atkinson, what have you been doing with yourself?"

"I went to Lords, sir, to see Middlesex play Lancashire, and I took my autograph book to get all their signatures, sir."

"And did you?" inquired Mr Carter.

"I got one, sir," said Atkinson proudly.

"And whose was that?"

"I'm not sure, sir, 'cos the chap's writing's a bit wobbly, and he just did a couple of squiggles and a flourish, and I didn't like to ask him what his name was," Atkinson confessed. "But if you look at it one way up it looks like B K Inman, and upside down it might be E J O'Reilly."

"And which do you think it really is?"

"Well, it's most probably Smith, sir, 'cos there wasn't an Inman or an O'Reilly in either of the teams, but there was a Smith on both sides," he explained, "so that makes it a two to one chance on its being one of them rather than anybody else, sir. But it's a pity his signature's so illiterate."

"Illegible," corrected Mr Carter.

"Oh, he must have been that, sir, 'cos even if he's not eligible for Middlesex, he would be for Lancashire, wouldn't he, sir, or he wouldn't be playing?"

Mr Carter was at a loss for the right answer to this one, so

4

he proceeded to shake hands all round, and furtively wiped the damp stickiness from his palm on his handkerchief. "Line up," he said, "I want your identity cards, health certificates, money for the bank and trunk keys."

Order was restored and Mr Carter started to check each boy's belongings. There were always snags in this. Temple had handed his identity card, as well as his ticket, to the collector at Victoria, and a hole had been punched in it before the error was discovered. Atkinson's father had departed to the city with his son's trunk key in his pocket; Venables' mother had lost his health certificate, but she sent a message to say that "it was all right, wasn't it?" – obviously trusting in Mr Carter's shrewd glance to detect any germs that might be lurking about her offspring.

"Right," said Mr Carter, "next boy."

"Me, sir, please, sir," said a voice.

Mr Carter's first meeting with Jennings was the routine affair of a busy master, who saw in front of him a small boy not unlike the dozens of other small boys who were lined up outside his room. His suit, socks and tie conformed exactly to the regulation pattern. His dark brown hair, which still bore the faintest trace of a parting, was no different from that of his fellows, and his face was the average sort of face worn by boys of his generation. So Mr Carter learned little from this first meeting. Later on, he was to learn a lot.

"A new boy, eh?" said Mr Carter. "And what's your name?"

"Jennings, sir."

"Oh, yes, here you are on the list. J C T Jennings; ten years, two months. Right?"

"No, sir, not quite right, sir; ten years, two months and three days last Tuesday, sir."

"We won't worry about that," said Mr Carter. He had placed the new boy by now. Only that morning the Headmaster had shown him a letter from a Mr Jennings, expressing doubts lest his son, who had never been away from home before, should not settle down at boarding school. Mr Carter gave him another look; he seemed the sort of boy who knew how to look after himself.

"We shall have to show you the ropes, shan't we?" said Mr Carter, sorting out the small pile of documents that Jennings placed before him.

"Identity card, yes; bank money, yes. Where's your health certificate?"

"I don't think I've got one of those, sir," said Jennings, not knowing what a health certificate looked like.

"You must have," returned Mr Carter with mock gravity. "How do we know you're not suffering from mumps, measles, chicken-pox, whooping cough, scarlet fever and bubonic plague?"

A look of alarm passed over Jennings' face. "I'm sure I'm not, sir," he said. "I haven't even got any spots, honestly, sir. Look, sir!"

"Isn't this it?" asked Mr Carter, extracting the certificate from Jennings' pocket and studying it. "Yes, I thought so. You're quite all right."

"Not even any bucolic plague?" asked Jennings, rather disappointed now that all was well.

"Not even a mump or a measle. That was just my little joke. Now we must get someone to show you round." His eyes searched the group clustered round the door.

"Come here, Venables," he said to an untidy looking boy of twelve.

"Yes, sir," said the untidy one.

"Come and be introduced. I want you to show Jennings the ropes. On my left," he proclaimed, in the manner of the best boxing referees, "on my left, Venables, easily distinguished by his trailing bootlaces."

"Oh, sir," protested Venables.

"On my right, Jennings, who's got to be looked after. Venables – Jennings: Jennings – Venables." As though to heighten this sporting comparison, a bell rang in the distance.

"There's the tea bell," said the self-styled referee. "Take Jennings to the dining-hall and treat him as you would your brother."

"Yes, sir," replied the trailer of bootlaces.

"On second thoughts, don't," added Mr Carter. "I've seen how you treat your brother. Look after him as you do yourself and he certainly won't starve."

"Oh, sir!" said Venables in aggrieved tones. One had to sound aggrieved at the heavy-handed pleasantries of the staff, but actually it was rather flattering to be picked out for such a distinction. He led Jennings away to wash his hands for tea.

Old Pyjams, the general factotum, was putting up clean towels in the wash-room. His name was Robinson and he was in his early twenties, but he had to be called Old Pyjams because his opposite number, Hawkins, the night watchman, was known as Old Nightie.

"You'll 'ave to do without soap," Old Pyjams told them, "I ain't got around to getting it out yet."

This was all to the good because, by trailing their fingers under the cold tap and pressing hard on the clean towels, the boys were able to make impressions which would have delighted the fingerprint department of Scotland Yard.

Another bell rang and Venables led Jennings to the dining-hall where Mr Carter was waiting to say grace. The buzz of conversation ceased.

"*Benedictus, benedicat*," said Mr Carter.

There was a scraping of chairs and the buzz broke out again.

"You'd better sit here, Jennings, next to this other new chap," said Venables. "Here, you, what's your name?"

"Charles Edwin Jeremy Darbishire," said the small edition of his father, in capital letters.

"You can keep the Charles Edwin Jeremy, you won't be needing it," said Venables. "And you'd better talk to Jennings as you're both new." And with the air of one who has already been overgenerous to small new fry, he turned to the sublime heights of conversation with his equals.

Jennings and Darbishire looked at each other without interest. Having been bidden to talk, neither could think of anything to say. Finally, Darbishire cleared his throat.

"Magnificent weather for September, isn't it?" he said in his best rectory drawing-room manner.

"Uh?" said Jennings, out of his depth in polite conversation. "Oh, yes. Super... I say," he went on, "how much cash have you got in the school bank? I've got a pound."

"I did have a pound," said Darbishire, "but I spent fourpence halfpenny on the way here this afternoon, so I've got – er – nineteen and – er – I've got a pound less fourpence halfpenny. I gave it to that master who said grace just now. What's his name?"

"I think he's Mr – er – I say Venables, what's that master's name?"

With an effort, Venables descended from the sublime to the ridiculous. "Were you talking to me?"

"Yes. That master. What did you say his name was?"

"That's Benedick," replied Venables. "We all call him that, anyway. Actually, his name's Mr Carter."

"Why call him something else?" demanded Jennings.

"Well, you heard him say grace just now. *Benedictus* and all that. And after meals he says, '*benedicto, benedicata*.' "

Jennings waited in case more explanation was forthcoming, but it wasn't.

"Go on," he said.

"I've just told you," said Venables with the patience reserved for imbeciles. "*Benedicata* – Benedick Carter."

"Oh," said Jennings. "Is that a joke?"

"You're a bit wet, aren't you?" replied Venables.

"It's Latin, Jennings," broke in the erudite Darbishire. "My father knows a lot of Latin. He's a clergyman, and he says – "

"Yes, but what does all that benedict – whatever it is, mean?" demanded Jennings.

"Don't ask me," said Venables. "I was thirteenth in Latin last term. I'll ask Bod; he's a brain." And calling to Temple on the opposite side of the table, he asked, "I say, Bod, there's a new chap here who wants to know what the grace means in English. You were first in Latin last term; you ought to know."

Temple, alias Bod, considered. When one is first in Latin, it doesn't do to confess ignorance. "Well," he said with an authoritative air, "when they say it before meals it means something like 'come and get it,' and after meals it means 'you've had it.' "

And having given the ignorant newcomers the benefit of his learning, he returned to his shepherd's pie.

"But if what Bod said is right – " Jennings began.

"You mustn't call him Bod," said Venables, shocked. "New chaps aren't allowed to call fairly senior chaps by their nicknames until their second term."

"Then his name isn't really Bod, any more than Mr Carter's name is Benedick," persisted Jennings, who liked to get things straight.

" 'Course not," said Venables. "His name's Temple, and his initials are CAT, so naturally we call him Dog."

"But you didn't call him Dog, you called him Bod," argued Jennings.

"Give a chap a chance to get a word in," said Venables. "I haven't finished yet. It's a bit of a sweat calling him Dog, so we call him Dogsbody for short."

"But it isn't short," protested Jennings. "Dogsbody's much longer than Dog."

"Okay, then," replied Venables logically, "it needs shortening. Bod short for Body, and Dogsbody short for Dog. Really!" And he shook his head, sadly. "You new oiks are dim at picking things up."

"It's a nickname, Jennings," said Darbishire. "My father says that the word 'nickname' is derived from the Anglo-Saxon word 'eke-name' which means 'also named,' and it's true, 'cos if you say 'an eke-name,' very quickly, it sort of turns itself into 'a nickname,' doesn't it?"

They practised turning eke-name into nickname until Jennings received a peremptory demand from Atkinson to "pass the ozard and stop hiccupping."

Jennings looked up and down the table, but could see nothing that answered to this description.

"What did you say you wanted?" he asked, helplessly.

"The ozard," repeated Atkinson, marvelling that new boys could be so stupid.

"I don't know what – oh, d'you mean the jam?" asked Jennings.

"Of course I do," said Atkinson, cutting his bread and butter into minute cubes. "What else could I mean?"

"Yes, I can see there's nothing else," said Jennings, "but why is it ozard?"

Atkinson, as a new boy, had asked exactly the same question less than a year before, but his manner implied that he had been born with preparatory school jargon on his lips.

"School jam's rotten muck," he explained. "It tastes like hair cream. Of course, all school food's muck, but usually it's pretty decent, so that makes it wizard muck, if you follow me."

Jennings followed him.

"Okay then," proceeded Atkinson. "You've heard of the Wizard of Oz, of course. Well, obviously, the opposite of wizard is ozard, isn't it?"

Jennings conceded the point.

"That shepherd's pie we've just had was supersonic muck so it's wizard, but this school jam's ghastly so it's ozard. Everything ghastly is ozard; being a new chap's pretty ozard for a bit, but you'll get used to it when you've been here as long as I have."

"And how long have you been here?" Jennings wanted to know.

"Me? Oh, I've been here donkeys' years. Ages and ages," said Atkinson, and his voice came from the mists of antiquity. "Well, two terms, anyway," he compromised.

After tea Venables escorted Jennings and Darbishire to a classroom, where some dozen boys were laboriously engaged in writing post-cards to let their parents know of their safe arrival.

"You wait here," said Venables. "If you haven't got a post-card, Old Wilkie'll give you one." With that he disappeared, leaving Jennings and Darbishire wondering which of the occupants of the room might be Old Wilkie.

Jennings approached the largest of the boys, who had finished writing his post-card and was dabbing the wet ink with his handkerchief in lieu of blotting paper.

"I say," said Jennings. "Are you Old Wilkie?"

The handkerchief paused in mid-blot.

"Am I Old Wilkie?" he said surprised. "Am I Old Wilkie?" And he went off into peals of laughter. "I say, you blokes," he gasped to the rest of the room when his laughter had

11

subsided slightly, "there's a character here who wants to know if I'm Old – ha-ha-ha-ha; he wants to know if I'm Old – hee-hee-hee-hee." And turning again to Jennings, he said, "No, I'm not," and resumed Operation Blotting with his handkerchief.

Neither Jennings nor Darbishire could see anything to laugh at, so they smiled politely and waited. A moment later the door handle rattled noisily, and the door hurtled open as though a small charge of dynamite had been placed behind it, and Old Wilkie burst in. Mr Wilkins was young and vigorous, the "Old" being merely a courtesy title. He was junior to Mr Carter and offered a complete contrast to him in every way; for Mr Carter remained quietly calm in the midst of the most frantic hurly-burly which occurs occasionally, even in the best regulated preparatory schools. But Mr Wilkins had none of his colleague's placidity. He hurtled and exploded his way through life like a radio-controlled projectile.

"I want everybody's post-cards, immediately," he boomed in a voice like a loud-hailer. "If you haven't finished, then you ought to have done. I can't wait all night. Lots to do."

"Please, sir, Darbishire and I haven't got any post-cards, sir," said Jennings.

"New boys, eh! Yes, of course you are; must be. Thought I hadn't seen your faces about the place before. Here you are," he went on; "two post-cards, two pens. Go and write them."

"Who do I have to write to, sir?" asked Darbishire.

"Not 'who,' 'whom,'" corrected Mr Wilkins. "To your mother and father, of course, who else?" He paused, considering whether he should have said "whom else."

Darbishire still looked puzzled.

"Well, go on," said Mr Wilkins. "Mother and father. No point in writing to the Archbishop of Canterbury; he won't

12

be interested. Tell them you've arrived safely."

"But they know that, sir," said Darbishire. "My father came down with me."

"Can't help that," said Mr Wilkins. "School rules say 'write post-card home.' All right then, write post-card home. Won't do any harm, will it?"

Jennings and Darbishire sat down at a desk. Darbishire sucked his pen while Jennings discovered, to his delight, that the inkwell was three-quarters full of ink-soaked blotting paper. With infinite care, he proceeded to fish for little bits with his nib and proudly displayed the results of his toil on the top of the desk, where the ink trickled down in little streams.

Darbishire decided to assure his parents that he was concerned about the state of their health. He headed his card, "*Linbury Court Preparatory School, Dunhambury, Sussex,*" in huge, sprawling writing that covered more than half the post-card. "*My dearest Mother and Father,*" he went on in letters half an inch high and nearly twice as broad, and discovered that there was only enough space left for one more line. "*I hope you are quite –*" He stopped, having completely filled up the available space. There was just room for a full stop, so he put that in and took his effort up for Mr Wilkins' approval.

Mr Wilkins adjusted his eyes to the outsize script and blinked.

"I hope you are quite – ?" he read out, bewildered. "I hope you are quite, what?"

"No, not quite what, sir," corrected Darbishire gently. "Quite well."

"So one might gather," expostulated Mr Wilkins. "But you haven't said that. You can't say 'I hope you are quite, full stop.' It's nonsense!"

"I hadn't got room for any more, sir," explained Darbishire.

"And it's all right, really, 'cos my father'll know by the full stop at the end that I'd finished and wasn't called away unexpectedly in the middle of anything, sir."

"But don't you see, you silly little boy, it doesn't make sense? How's your father going to know what it is "quite" that you hope he is? For all he knows, you might be going to say you hope he's quite – " Mr Wilkins was unable to think of a suitable comparison.

"But it's bound to mean quite 'well,' sir," reasoned Darbishire. "After all, you guessed it, and if you can, sir, I'm sure my father could, and I wouldn't be likely to mean I hope you're quite 'ill,' would I, sir?"

Mr Carter would probably have sighed. Mr Wilkins made a noise like an inner tube exploding under pressure. The back of his neck turned pink and he closed his eyes and breathed deeply. After a short period of convalescence, he opened his eyes and gave Darbishire another post-card.

Jennings had finished Operation Salvage in the inkpot and was gnawing the end of his pen. It would take a week or so to chew his way down to the nib, he decided, but already the pen showed signs of giving way as the end was beginning to spray out like a paintbrush. The noise of Mr Wilkins' mental anguish recalled him to the realms of scholarship, and he set about collecting material for his literary masterpiece.

A post-card home was something new in his experience. What should he say? His mother had told him to be sure to pay his pound into the school bank as soon as he arrived. He could say he had done that, for a start. He was richer than Darbishire because he had only got a pound less fourpence halfpenny. What else? Well, there was that frightfully funny joke Mr Carter had made about his having bubonic plague. What was it they called Mr Carter? Benny something? And it had something to do with the grace that Bod could translate, because he was a brain at Latin. Oh, yes, and that shepherd's pie for tea had been lovely. Surely he had enough material now for his post-card. He wrote:

"*Dear Mother,*
    "I gave mine in to Mr cater Darbsher has spend 4½ of his my healthser ticket was in my pocket he said I had got bubnick plag it was a jok he is called Benny Dick toe I think it is. We had ozard of wiz for tea Atkion says wiz is good and oz is garstly so do I. Love John.
    "PS. Temple is a brain, he is short for dogs boody."

Pleased with his effort, he trotted up to Mr Wilkins and awaited his approval.

Mr Wilkins did his best to decipher the message. As a solver of crossword puzzles, he felt that if only he had a clue, he might be able to read what appeared to be an ingenious code. But Mr Wilkins hadn't a clue and this time, his period of convalescence was longer.

The dormitory bell was ringing an hour later when Mr Wilkins reluctantly accepted Jennings' post-card. It was his seventh attempt and Mr Wilkins knew what it meant because Jennings, with infinite patience, had explained it. But to Mr and Mrs Jennings, who had no interpreter to help them, the post-card's message remained forever a mystery.

2

Trouble Looms Ahead

"You sleep in this bed, Jennings," said Venables, "and you're next to him here, Darbishire. Go on, you've only got ten minutes to get into bed."

The dormitory was a small one. There were five beds, with a chair beside each; three washbasins by the window and a large mirror in a dark corner of the room.

Jennings was still enthralled by the novelty of this new method of living one's life, but to Darbishire, the sparse furnishing of the dormitory compared unfavourably with the comfort of his bedroom at home, and the sight of his pyjamas, sponge bag and Bible lying on his hard iron bed in this unfamiliar room was too much. He gulped twice and swallowed hard.

"What on earth's the matter with you, Darbishire?" asked Temple.

"Nothing," said Darbishire through misty spectacles. "Well, nothing much, except I don't like this place. When I'm at home my father always comes and talks to me when I'm in bed and – well, it's all so different here, isn't it?"

"Oh, I don't know," said Jennings philosophically, "we'll probably get used to it in three or four years."

"You'll have a smash-on lot to get used to," said Venables. "Wait till you get into the Head's Latin class; it's spivish

16

ozard, isn't it, Atki?"

"Yes, rather," said Atkinson ghoulishly. "He made me write out the passive of 'Audio' twenty-five times once; it nearly killed me."

"And if you stop," added Temple, determined to make the worst of it, "if you take a breath even, when you're going through a verb, you get a stripe. I got fifty-seven stripes for Latin last term and I'm the best in the form."

Darbishire paled slightly, but Jennings was undaunted.

"What are the other masters like?" he demanded.

Venables, Temple, and Atkinson considered. They were all very happy at Linbury; they all liked the masters, and they knew that the rules of the school were made for their own good and for their own enjoyment. But one couldn't possibly admit all this, and only by making out that the school was one degree removed from a concentration camp, and that the school rules would have been condemned by the Spanish Inquisition on compassionate grounds – only by such colouring of the truth could one hope to avoid cramping one's style, and hold the attention of an audience.

"Old Wilkie's pretty ozard," said Temple, twirling a sock round his head autogyrically. "Sometimes he's double that – that's ozard squared. And when he's in a rare bate, he's been known to touch ozard cubed, in five-second bursts." And standing on his bed, he proceeded to give an impersonation of Mr Wilkins in the grip of ozardry, raised to the power of three.

"I – I – I – you – you – you – corwumph!" he spluttered. In point of fact, it was nothing like Mr Wilkins, but the audience were not fussy about minor details of characterisation and applauded vigorously. "Come here, Temple – you miserable specimen!" continued the impersonator. "You – you – crawling earthworm! You pestilential buffoon! You – you – don't you know that the angles at the base of an

17

isosceles triangle are jolly nearly equal? Write it out a hundred and fifty million times before tea." And, flushed with pride at the appreciative way in which his act was received, he hurled his pullover into space and attacked Venables with a few friendly straight lefts and short jabs to the body.

Darbishire disentangled himself from Temple's pullover, which had descended upon him, and felt even worse than he had done before.

"Do you mean he gets angry?" he asked with growing concern.

"We call it breezy," replied Atkinson. "And sometimes there's such a super-duper breeze that the windows rattle. It's wizard – well, it is if it's somebody else he's in a bate with and not you," he added as an afterthought.

"What's Mr Carter like?" demanded Jennings.

"Oh, Benedick's all right," said Venables. "He's a bit crackers at times, but all masters are, anyway. It's probably a law of their union."

The boxing bout had ended as suddenly as it had begun and Venables felt it was time he took a hand in describing the joys of school life.

"Now what else have you got to know?" he went on. "First, you mustn't put your hands in your pockets, unless you're a prefect."

"Why?" asked Jennings.

"I don't know! It's just a rule."

"Supposing I want my handkerchief?" asked Darbishire. "It'll be years before I'm a prefect, if ever, and I can't sniff all that time, and my father said that if my catarrh gets – "

"You know what I mean," said Venables. "You mustn't strut about with your hands in your pockets as though you owned the place. And you mustn't run in the corridors; you mustn't use fountain pens; you mustn't play conkers in the

Assembly Hall; you mustn't read comics; you mustn't eat tuck before lunch; you mustn't wear your vest for football and you mustn't wear your cap like a spiv."

"You are allowed to breathe without special permission, though," added Temple, graciously putting in a good word for the authorities.

Venables had stopped, unable to think of any more "mustn'ts." But he was not defeated for long.

"Oh, yes," he added, making up a new rule on the spur of the moment. "If you make a duck in a house match or let a goal through, your name'll be Mud for the rest of the term."

"But I always do make a duck," lamented Darbishire. "I'm no good at games."

"That's all right, Darbishire," said Jennings. "I'll give you some coaching. I've seen the Australians play, so there's not much about how to play cricket that I don't know."

"Don't swank, Jennings," said Temple. "I don't suppose you know anything, really, and it'd be much easier to call Darbishire 'Mud,' anyway; it's shorter."

The discussion was interrupted by a bell ringing in the distance. "Gosh!" said Atkinson. "That's the five minutes bell. Come on, let's get washed."

There was a frantic scurry of undressing; small clusters of clothes blossomed on the floor in untidy heaps. Later on, the topmost garment would be picked up and folded tidily to shroud the multitude of unsightly sins that lay beneath. But now Operation Ablution claimed their attention. Five boys into three wash-basins works out at an impractical fraction, so tradition required that the old hands should wash first, while the recruits swelled the ranks of the great unwashed until their turn came.

Atkinson dashed wildly to his basin, turned on the tap and rushed madly back to his bed for his sponge bag. His speed was largely wasted, because he had forgotten to put the plug in and, on his return, the basin was as empty as when he had left it.

Venables gave the impression of haste by a series of horizontal and vertical leaps over and across the beds, but he kept missing his footing and wasted time returning to the airfield for a fresh take-off. But soon a few damp patches behind the ears denoted that he, too, was washing.

Temple hastened to retrieve his pyjama jacket from the top of the electric light shade, whence he had hurled it in his attempts to make his impersonation of Mr Wilkins seem more life-like.

But Darbishire, who was not yet used to having his bedtime regulated by bells, sat on his bed and tugged forlornly at a knot in his shoelaces.

"Oh, and there's another thing, Jennings," said Venables amidst splashes, "you have to wash your feet every night unless it's your bath night."

He grabbed his toothpaste and squeezed hard. "Oh, golly!" he said. "This is ozard muck. Look, I've squeezed out about a yard and a half. What'll I do with it? I can't put it back."

"You could write your name round the basin like they do with icing sugar," said Jennings, who had arrived to occupy the remaining basin. "Have you got enough to write 'many happy returns of the day?' "

"Haven't got time," replied Venables, "though it'd be quite a prang if we'd thought of it earlier." He took a mouthful from his tooth glass and gargled.

"I say, Atki," he said, "can you change gear when you gargle? Like this, look – I mean, listen."

He gargled again, starting on a low note and rising up the scale with forcible vocal contortions to show where the gears changed from low to second, from second to top. The car gathered speed and, as an artistic finale, faded into the distance.

"Super duper!" said Jennings.

"Smash-on prang!" agreed Atkinson.

"Yes, it's not bad, is it?" admitted Venables. "I've been practising quite a lot in the hols."

"All the same, I can do it just as well," said Jennings.

"So can I," said Atkinson.

The dormitory hummed with cars changing gear; light sports cars with super-charged engines and heavy lorries stalling on steep hills. Atkinson swallowed his gargle while changing down to take a hairpin bend, at eighty miles per hour, and had to be slapped on the back by his fellow motorists.

"I know something better than that," said Jennings. "I can be a super-jet fighter; listen... Eee-ow-ow; eee-ow-ow; eee-ow-ow... Dacka-dacka; dacka-dacka..." His machine gun spat venomously. "Eee-ow-ow; eee-ow-ow; eee-ow-ow... Doyng!"

"What's the 'doyng'?" inquired Venables.

"That's the other plane crashing after I've hit him," said the aeronaut. "I'm going into a dive, now. Eee-ow-ow; eee-ow-ow... Dacka-dacka; dacka-dacka..."

The Squadron's personnel was at once joined by Venables, Atkinson and Temple in Spitfires, and all four eee'd and ow'd and dacka-dacka'd and doynged with outstretched arms, wheeling, banking and diving, while Darbishire sat on his bed and put his fingers in his ears.

The door opened and the noise stopped abruptly. "H'm," said Mr Carter from the doorway. "If dorm No. 4 Fighter Squadron doesn't make a forced landing and get back to base, there'll be trouble; this light's going out in three minutes."

"Yes, sir," murmured the Fighter Squadron meekly.

The door closed on Mr Carter.

"Come on, you chaps, get a move on," said Venables. "Benedick means it when he says – " He broke off, his eye affronted by a shocking disregard for tradition. "Here, Jennings," he thundered indignantly, "what are you doing at that basin?"

"Washing," said Jennings. "You said I'd got to wash my feet."

"But you can't have that basin first; it's Bod's. He bagged it last term; new chaps have to wash last."

"Well, I'm here now," said Jennings.

Temple came rushing across to defend his rights.

"That's my basin, Jennings. Get out," he ordered.

"Well, I didn't know," said Jennings.

"You jolly well ought to know. Go on; get out of the way."

Jennings refused to be cowed. "I was here first, so I'm going to wash first," he said.

"I wouldn't stand that from a new chap, Bod," said Venables. "It's just super-hairy cheek."

" 'Course it is," put in Atkinson, "and spivish disloyal to the dorm rules."

"Don't worry," said Temple. "I'm not going to stand for any ozard oik of a new chap telling me what to do. I'm going to count three, Jennings, and if you don't get out, I'll squeeze this wet sponge down your pyjamas."

Jennings didn't like the situation much. Temple was easily the largest boy in the room and his allies stood on either hand, like Herminius and Spurius Lartius assisting Horatius in the brave days of old. Still, Jennings remembered, his father had told him to stick up for himself; he decided to try it.

"You can go and chase yourself, Temple," he said, as that worthy was mouthing "Three" in menacing tones.

"All right then," said Temple, and squeezed the sponge.

The water was cold and uncomfortable, and Jennings let out a piercing scream, which echoed all over the building, and dissolved into tears.

"You soaked me," wailed Jennings. "I'm all wringing wet!"

"Cave, Benedick!" said Atkinson with an eye on the opening door.

Mr Carter sized up the situation.

"Who was responsible for that screaming noise?" he asked.

"I was, sir. It was Bod's fault, sir; Temple, I mean," gulped Jennings between sobs. "He squeezed a wet sponge down the back of my pyjama trousers and made me all wet."

"Sneak!" hissed Atkinson and Venables in tones which they mistakenly supposed were too soft for Mr Carter's adult ear.

"Jennings, you don't quite understand," said Mr Carter. "I didn't say who 'made' that noise, I asked who was 'responsible' for its being made; that gives the culprit a chance to own up without laying the victim open to the charge of telling tales; there's a difference you see."

"Yes, sir," said Jennings.

"Perhaps I'm still a trifle deaf from those aircraft noises you were making, and I didn't quite catch the answer to my question! Now, who was responsible for those screams?"

"I was, sir," admitted the defender of tradition.

"Thank you, Temple. We'll go into the merits of the case in the morning. Come and see me after breakfast."

"Yes, sir," said Temple.

"We'll have silence now while you get into bed – and get a move on," Mr Carter said.

He waited while they washed.

Temple, seething with indignation at Jennings' treachery, hurtled into bed hoping that the ferocity of his manner would show Jennings what he felt about him.

Darbishire, unaccustomed to getting a move on, prepared

for a lengthy getting-ready-for-bed ceremony which Mr Carter had to cut short. He folded up Darbishire's clothes for him and waited while he read his prescribed ten verses from the New Testament; then he switched off the light.

"Good night, everybody," he said.

Temple waited long enough for Mr Carter to reach the end of the passage; then he whispered, "You ruinous little sneak, Jennings. You wait! I'll bash you up tomorrow."

"Good Old Bod," said Atkinson in the same low tone. "Do it before tea, that's the best time."

"It wasn't my fault," protested Jennings loudly.

"Sh! Sh!" came from the three old-timers. "We're on silence. That means whisper."

"Benedick's got supersonic ear-sight," said Venables. "He can hear you even when he's downstairs."

"Well, it wasn't my fault," repeated Jennings in what was meant for a whisper.

" 'Course it was," said Temple. "You needn't have yelled your head off like that, you great baby."

"Sorry, Temple," said Jennings.

"All right," said Temple ungraciously; "but don't do it again."

For a first-class bashing-up to peter out in apologies was not Venables' idea of a fitting climax. He decided to stir things up again. "You're not going to let it go at that, Bod, are you?" he asked. "After all, even Benedick knew Jennings was in the wrong, 'cos he ticked him off for sneaking."

"Okay, then," said Temple. "We'll have the bashing-up, as arranged."

Darbishire felt himself constrained to speak.

"That's Not Fair," he protested in capital letters. "You've accepted Jennings' apology, so it's not a square deal if you bash him up now."

"I can if I feel like it," said Temple.

"My father says you should never go back on your word," persisted the champion of the square deal.

"Shut up, Darbishire, you hairy ruin; nobody asked you," put in Venables.

"Any more from you, Darbishire," said Temple, "and I'll bash you up tomorrow, when I've finished with Jennings. And you can tell your father so with my love."

Silence reigned for a few moments, until it occurred to Atkinson that the maximum enjoyment could be wrung from the situation only if Jennings was made to realise just what was in store for him.

"I say, Jennings," he said. "Temple won the school boxing championship last term. Oh, boy! Oh, boy! What a smash-on bashing-up it's going to be! Rare! Super-duper! And wizzo!"

"I don't care," said Jennings, caring very much.

"Well, I don't think it's fair – " began Darbishire.

"Shut up, Darbishire, nobody asked you," said the three old-timers in unison.

"You know, Jennings," proceeded Atkinson, warming to his task, "you're taking on a big job when you get on the wrong side of Bod; he's hefty daring. Why, d'you know what he did last term? He foxed into town on a bus, and there's a super-lethal punishment for foxing."

Atkinson went on to explain that this notorious feat, which had placed Temple on the dizziest pedestal of fame, had occurred one half-holiday. Quietly slipping away from Mr Wilkins' cricket practice, Temple had taken a bus into the town and had gone to Valenti's, a sweet shop which specialised in the manufacture of Brighton rock.

"And he brought back sixpenny-worth of rock in a bag with the shop's name on to prove he'd been," ended the narrator in admiring tones.

"And I wasn't caught, either," put in the hero of the

exploit. He glowed with pride at the mention of his heroism and determined to make a little more hay while the sun still shone. "That's the sort of chap I am, really," he said, with becoming modesty. "Of course, it's quite easy if you've got the nerve."

The audience murmured their appreciation.

"Still," he went on, reluctant to leave the topic, "no one else has ever done it. There's no one, except me, who'd dare to, I suppose. Well, good night, chaps," said the great one, condescendingly. "Oh, Atki, remind me to bash Jennings before tea tomorrow, just in case I forget."

Neither Jennings nor Darbishire realised that, ninety-nine times out of a hundred, these threats are never carried out. They have to be uttered, of course, to restore the shattered pride of anyone who imagines that he has been wronged, but before the penalty can be exacted, the insult has usually been forgotten and the protagonists have become close friends. In the present instance, the three old-stagers were not contemplating a gruesome outcome to their threat; they were merely administering a mild rebuke to Jennings, so that he might know his lowly station in life and not get above himself. Unaware that such face-saving procedure is merely a matter of form, Darbishire's feelings of fair play were outraged.

"It's not fair," he protested.

"And if Darbishire starts getting uppish I'll do him as well," said Temple.

"I wouldn't like to be you tomorrow, Jennings," shuddered Venables, with relish.

"I couldn't care less," replied Jennings. In point of fact, he couldn't have cared more, but he wasn't going to let anyone know. He tried to remember what his father had said about standing up for himself. Perhaps if he stood up for himself really well, he might even... He fell asleep.

Darbishire lay awake with black despair in his soul. Whatever sort of a place was this that his father had so mistakenly sent him to? He had no idea that school was a place where life was governed by clanging bells and threats of being bashed up; where the rules were thwarting and masters made you write things out a hundred and fifty million times. Golly! However long would that take? Well, suppose it took you a minute to write it out once, that meant sixty times an hour and there were twenty-four hours in a day. So that made... Gosh! But you would have to stop to eat, wouldn't you? He tried again. After his third calculation, when the answer came to slightly more than forty-seven years, he fell asleep.

3

Jennings Gains a Reputation

Jennings had only the haziest recollection of the events of the following morning. It seemed as though he spent the time in getting into long lines which moved somewhere whenever a bell sounded. Where the line went he wasn't sure, but the manoeuvre always ended up by a master asking him his name and how old he was. After that, the master would give him some exercise books, or a pair of football socks or some other suitable memento of the occasion.

As a party game it had its points, but as the presents were rather dull, he was glad when lunch time came. But this proved to be only a short respite for, after the meal was over, bells clanged again and everybody started to line up for another bout of to-ing and fro-ing.

Jennings had had enough, so he slipped unobtrusively out of the line as it rounded a corner and wandered off by himself. Remembering Temple's threat, he had a vague idea of keeping out of the way until tea-time when, perhaps, the danger would be passed. At the far end of the quad he discovered Darbishire all by himself.

"What are you doing here, Darbishire?" he demanded. "You ought to be marching about somewhere in a long line."

"I know," replied Darbishire, gulping visibly. Jennings

could not see his eyes because of his spectacles, but streaks of grime down his cheeks told their own story.

"I say, Darbishire, you haven't been crying, have you?" asked Jennings.

"N-no, not really. I've just been wishing I was at home, and it's made my glasses go all misty."

"You've got nothing to worry about," Jennings consoled him. "How about me? I'm due for a bashing-up before tea."

"Well, so am I, if I get uppish," Darbishire replied.

"And have you been getting uppish?"

"No, I've been feeling downish all morning." And in a burst of confidence, he added: "I don't like boarding school; everything sounds so awful, and – oh, I wish I'd never come!"

"Well, I'm not feeling too good, either," said Jennings. "I do wish I could see my father for a few minutes, so's he could tell me the best thing to do during bashing-ups; there's probably something you can do, if you know what."

"Oh, dear, I'm so miserable," lamented Darbishire. "My father says we should always strive to – "

"I say," said Jennings, as a brilliant thought struck him. "I say, Darbishire, I've got an idea! Shall we run away?"

"Run away?" gasped Darbishire, stunned by the boldness of the idea.

"Yes; go home. Then you can tell your father you don't like it here, and my father can tell me how to stand up for myself against the school boxing champion."

"But how can we run away?" objected the law-abiding Darbishire. "We're not allowed out!"

Jennings dismissed the trifling objection with a shrug of the shoulders.

"We could just walk down the drive and get a bus to the station and go home. And we could ask Mr Carter for our pounds out of the bank, so's we could buy our tickets."

"But I've only got nineteen and something."

"That'll be masses to buy a ticket with," Jennings assured him. "I say, it'll be super exciting, won't it?"

Darbishire wasn't at all sure that he was cut out for that sort of excitement. "S'pose we get caught?" he asked anxiously.

Jennings considered. It was, of course, quite a point. Perhaps there was some way of reducing the risk.

"I know," he said after deep thought; "we could disguise ourselves. Then, perhaps, even if they saw us, we wouldn't be recognised."

"What, beards and false noses and things?" gasped Darbishire.

"Yes," said Jennings, as though the donning of disguise was an everyday occurrence with him.

"But I haven't got a beard," objected the practical Darbishire. "And, anyway, I'd look silly wearing a beard with short trousers."

Jennings wasn't going to let minor objections interfere with what promised to be a first-rate scheme.

"Well, p'r'aps not beards, then," he conceded; "but I could wear your glasses, that'd be something, and you could – er – "

What could Darbishire have?

"You could – you could walk with a limp!" he decided in a flash of genius.

For the first time since he had arrived at school, Darbishire began to enjoy himself. The idea of walking with a limp cheered him up enormously.

"Coo! Yes! Wizzo!" he said, all sorrows forgotten. "Like this, look!" And with staggering gait he hobbled round in small circles.

"You look more like a crab with chilblains," said Jennings. He began to feel he had been over-generous in giving

30

Darbishire a role so rich in theatrical possibilities. "No, bags I walk with the limp," he amended; "I can do it better than you."

"That's not fair," protested Darbishire. "You said I could have it; besides, you're going to have my glasses, so there won't be anything for me."

"Well, you won't be wearing your glasses," Jennings argued.

"But it isn't a disguise just to be not wearing something."

"Well," conceded Jennings, "you can carry a stick and turn your collar up."

"Coo! Yes! And wear my sun hat with a dent in the top like a trilby," said Darbishire happily. "We must remember not to wear our school caps, mustn't we, 'cos that'd spoil the disguise."

"Come on, let's go and find Mr Carter and ask for our money," said Jennings, and, full of excited optimism, they dashed wildly into the building and up the stairs to Mr Carter's study.

As they were about to knock on his door, Darbishire thought of a brilliant amendment to the plan.

"I say, Jennings," he said, "couldn't we both walk with a limp?"

Mr Carter looked up from his desk. "Hallo," he said. "What do you two want?"

"We want some money from the bank, please, sir."

"How. much?" inquired Mr Carter.

"I want a pound, and Darbishire wants nineteen and whatever it is he's got."

"That's rather a lot, isn't it? What do you want it for?"

This was a difficult question.

"Do we have to say what it's for, sir?" asked Jennings.

"Well, a large sum of money like that's a bit unusual. I'm afraid I can't let you have it unless you tell me why."

Darbishire decided that the game was up, but Jennings was made of sterner stuff.

"Please, sir," he asked, "how much could we have without having to tell you what it's for, sir?"

"I shouldn't be curious up to about sixpence," said Mr Carter generously.

"Oh... Well, if that's all, can we have sixpence each, then, sir?"

Mr Carter gave it to them. "You won't spend it on anything foolish, will you?" he remarked.

Mr Carter smiled as the door closed on the two conspirators. He already had an idea that something was afoot and decided to hold a watching brief. In Mr Carter's experience it did not pay to nip enterprises in the bud too early, as they had a habit of bursting out again in other directions. He opened the door and followed at a discreet distance.

On the far side of the quad Jennings and Darbishire held another council of war.

Well, I s'pose that's that," said Darbishire philosophically. "And I was feeling quite excited about walking with a limp with my collar turned up; I was going to try and look like 'Dick Barton.' Of course, I know I wouldn't look like him really, in school socks – but that sort of chap. Still," he ended lugubriously, "it's all a wash-out, now."

"No, it isn't," said the irrepressible Jennings. "We've got sixpence each; that's enough to get to the station on the bus."

"But what about train fares?"

"We'll go by taxi," said Jennings in a lordly manner. "We'll get one at the station and my father'll pay when we get there. I live at Haywards Heath. It's only about fifteen miles away."

But Darbishire lived in Hertfordshire and thought it would cost at least a hundred pounds to get there by taxi. Jennings had the answer. They would go to Haywards Heath where Mr

Jennings, having paid for the taxi, would lend Darbishire enough money to get home by train. With Mr Jennings' co-operation taken for granted, the scheme appeared flawless.

The coast was clear. Sounds of activity from the Assembly Hall indicated that the main body of the school was busily engaged in some communal pursuit.

"Come on, then," said Jennings, "give me your glasses and turn your collar up."

"Gosh, Darbishire," he continued when the spectacles were in position, "your eyesight must be rotten – I mean ozard. I can't see a thing with them."

"Well, I can't see a thing without them," complained Darbishire, peering shortsightedly in all directions.

The transfer of the spectacles had reduced visibility to ten-tenths fog for both of them and they were unaware that Mr Carter was an interested spectator of their departure. Groping blindly and limping heavily, their sun hats pulled low over their brows, they proceeded down the drive in a series of furtive staggers. Though disguised to the hilt, Mr Carter had no difficulty in recognising them, though he was slightly puzzled as to why they found it necessary to walk as though they were in the last stages of intoxication.

In this manner they passed through the school gates and on to the road. Fortunately, there was no one about, as their antics would have invited investigation by any kindly soul whose heart is wrung by the sight of small boys in physical agony.

"We turn right to get into the town," whispered Jennings in conspiratorial accents; "I remember it from yesterday. And I think there's a bus stop somewhere along here."

For fifty yards they stumbled uncertainly; then Jennings bumped into an obstruction which loomed up suddenly before his hazy gaze.

"I beg your pardon," he apologised to a post marked "Bus Stop," and again they moved on.

After a while Jennings stopped. "I can't go on wearing your glasses any longer, Darbishire," he said, "they're giving me a headache, and we must be nearly at the bus stop by now."

Darbishire put on his glasses.

"Yes, there it is," he exclaimed, "about twenty yards back; we've walked right past it. I can see it quite plainly now."

"So can I," said Jennings. It would be humiliating to confess that he had just apologised to it by mistake. "Come on, let's go back and wait for a bus. And if anyone comes along, we can nip behind the hedge."

"D'you think we need go on limping?" said Darbishire as they neared the bus stop. "It's smash-on tiring and there's no one about, anyway."

"Okay," said Jennings. "And we needn't talk in whispers either, as there's no one coming. Oh, golly! There is!" he gasped. "It's a man; he's coming out of the school gates. Quick! Get down behind the hedge!"

They hurled themselves behind the inadequate cover of the hedge and waited breathlessly.

"Who is it?" whispered Darbishire, and then spoilt the secrecy of the whisper with a loud yell. "Ow!" he wailed.

"Shut up, you fool!" hissed Jennings.

"But I'm kneeling on a nettle," groaned Darbishire.

"Keep your head down, you goof, or he'll see us!" He peered cautiously through a gap in the hedge. "Oh, heavens!" he gasped. "It's Mr Carter and he's coming this way. Lie down and don't move."

Mr Carter strolled slowly along towards the bus stop. Portions of small boy were visible through gaps in the hedge, but he affected not to notice. He was more than curious to know what the plan was, but he knew that if he were to

34

discover the boys so early in the proceedings, he probably never would know. They would merely stand uncomfortably on one foot and remain silent in the face of questions. No, he decided, the only way to find out how those minds were really working was to play the comedy out a bit longer. He walked passed the bus stop and disappeared round a bend in the road.

As the footsteps receded in the distance, Jennings cautiously raised his head.

"He's gone," he whispered triumphantly. "Jolly wizard job he didn't see us, wasn't it?"

"Are you sure he didn't?" inquired Darbishire anxiously.

" 'Course not; we crouched down, didn't we? Well, then, he couldn't have, possibly."

"Good," said Darbishire; "I think I'll get off my nettle now if you don't mind."

In the distance they heard a bus approaching.

The bus was a single-decker Southdown and it stopped in response to the frantic signals of the two boys. It was fairly full, but two seats in the front were vacant, and a man seated near the entrance alighted as Jennings and Darbishire, with anxious glances down the road, hopped quickly on to the platform and made for the front seats.

"You needn't go on limping, now," said Jennings, as Darbishire lurched forward with the sudden starting of the bus. "We'll be passing Mr Carter in a minute," he continued, "so we'll have to crouch down very low in our seats; then he won't see us. Isn't this fun?"

But the fun ceased some five seconds later when the bus slowed down.

"What are we stopping for?" asked Darbishire, "we've only just started."

"I'll have a recce," said Jennings, raising his eyes cautiously to the level of the window.

The sight that met his gaze chilled the blood in his veins; Mr Carter was standing in the road with hand upraised to stop the bus.

Mr Carter took the seat next to the entrance and carefully avoided looking at the front seats. Indeed, they appeared to be empty, for Jennings and Darbishire were crouching so low that nothing was visible. From a vantage point, some two feet from the ground, Jennings essayed a furtive reconnaissance.

"He's sitting right at the back," he reported in a whisper, "and he hasn't seen us."

"Oh, golly, we shouldn't have done this," groaned Darbishire. "There'll be an awful row. My father says, 'Oh, what a tangled web we weave – ' "

"He's looking out of the window. If those two fat ladies don't get off, he won't know we're here. What were you saying?"

"I was saying, 'Oh, what a tangled web we weave, when first we practise to deceive.' "

"Oh, shut up," retorted Jennings. "Here we are, in the middle of the most frantic jam and you start spouting proverbs!"

"Sorry, Jen," said Darbishire humbly. "It's only what my father – "

"Listen," whispered Jennings, "we'll go on crouching like this, and keep our heads down till Mr Carter gets off; then, we'll be all right."

"Yes, but s'posing he – " objected Darbishire.

"Fares, please!" said the conductor.

This was going to be a ticklish manoeuvre. Doubled up as they were, they had difficulty in getting their sixpences out of their trouser pockets, and the conductor was tapping his foot on the floor impatiently by the time they had succeeded.

"Two halves to the station," whispered Jennings inaudibly.

"Eh?" said the conductor. "Speak up, I can't 'ear yer."

"Two halves to the station, please," said Jennings, not daring to raise his voice.

"What's the matter, chum, laryngitis?" asked the conductor.

"Yes," croaked Jennings hoarsely.

"Can't yer pal talk neither? Where you going, son?" he boomed at Darbishire in a voice of thunder, as though the question might supply enough volume for the answer.

Darbishire's lips framed the word "Station," but no sound came. At the third attempt the conductor's lip-reading improved, and light dawned.

"Oh, station!" he said. "Well, why didn't yer say so? Two sore throats to the station – tanner each. I thenkyow." He punched their tickets and returned to the rear platform.

Several times the bus stopped. Passengers came and went, but Mr Carter remained; the combined wishful thinking of Jennings and Darbishire was quite unable to budge him. Three times new passengers advanced to the front seat, believing it to be empty, and were startled by the crouching figures who mimed at them to go away.

At every stop Jennings made a cautious survey. Surely he would get off soon, but by now, they had reached the town and Mr Carter was still sitting next to the exit. No amount of limping and trying to look like "Dick Barton" could deceive him at so close a range.

The bus stopped again.

"Station! Station!" called the conductor. "Hurry along, please!"

"Oh, golly! What shall we do?" moaned Darbishire.

"We'll just have to go a bit farther," said Jennings.

The conductor was anxious to be helpful. "Station!" he

yelled down the bus. "Hey, chum, didn't yer want the station? Oi!" And he whistled shrilly at the seemingly empty front seats.

"Don't take any notice," whispered Jennings. "Pretend you haven't heard."

But the conductor was not to be put off.

"You lads deaf as well as dumb?" he inquired, approaching.

"We – we're going a bit farther," murmured Jennings.

"Okay," said the conductor, ringing the bell. "How far are yer going?"

"I – I don't know yet. I hope to know soon."

The conductor scratched his head. The Company's Regulations did not say how one should deal with passengers who folded themselves up and mouthed at you and hoped to know their destination in the near future.

"Better drop yer at the 'ospital," he decided, "and get them sore throats looked at; that'll be a tuppeny."

"Oh, goodness," said Darbishire, "we haven't got any more money."

"Oh!" said the conductor. "You'll 'ave to get orf then, won't yer?"

"But we can't get off," urged Jennings desperately. "You don't understand. Look, couldn't you give me your address and I'll send the fare on to you."

"I've 'eard that one before," said the conductor. "Well, come on. Are yer going to 'ave another ticket or ain't yer?"

Darbishire was on the verge of tears and even Jennings' resource was not equal to the situation.

"No, no. Wait a minute," he implored.

"I ain't got all day," replied the conductor, "either yer – "

"Can I be of any assistance?" inquired Mr Carter politely.

"Oh, gosh!" said Jennings.

"Oh, golly!" said Darbishire.

Mr Carter gave them a friendly smile.

"It's these lads, sir; acting a bit queer. They're either ill or barmy or trying to get a free ride. I want another tuppence from both of them."

Mr Carter handed over the money.

"Would you mind stopping?" he said to the conductor. "I think we've all gone quite far enough."

They alighted in a silence that could be felt, and the two boys stood dejectedly on the pavement as the bus proceeded on its way.

"And now we'll have to catch a bus going the other way," said Mr Carter. "I'm glad you've got your glasses back again, Darbishire; you looked quite lost without them."

"Oh, sir. D'you mean you saw us?" asked Jennings incredulously.

"I'm afraid I couldn't help it," said Mr Carter. "And next time you hide behind a hedge, remember it's useless to put your head down if you leave your other end sticking up."

"Will there be an awful row, sir?" inquired Darbishire.

"Oh! I don't know," was the reply, "we all make mistakes. The best thing to do is to try and profit by them."

"But shan't we be expelled, sir?" persisted Darbishire.

"Why, would you mind very much?"

"I – I'd rather like it, sir," he confessed.

"I thought that was the trouble," said Mr Carter. "We all start off by feeling homesick; it's just one of those things which has to be mastered."

He assured Darbishire that there would not be a row. But this didn't help Jennings, as the return to school meant that the bashing-up would have to be faced after all.

Mr Carter sensed that all was not well.

"Well, Jennings?" he asked. "Is there anything else wrong?"

"Yes, sir," said Jennings. "If I go back now, I'm – oh – "

"Yes?"

"I can't tell you, sir. It'd be sneaking and you said last night we oughtn't to do that, sir."

"I think Jennings ought to tell you, sir," said Darbishire. "My father says that – "

"No. I can't," said Jennings, "and you can't make me, sir, 'cos of what you said about never listening to people who tell tales."

It is sometimes difficult for a master to draw the line between sneaking and genuine complaints, so Mr Carter suggested that perhaps Jennings could find his own salvation. Jennings was doubtful, but refused to reveal the cause of his troubles, and decided to go back to school and face them.

Mr Carter went down the road to inquire the time of the next bus back.

"I say, Darbishire," said Jennings when the master was out of earshot, "he's, jolly decent, really, isn't he?"

"Yes," agreed Darbishire. "I thought he'd kick up no end of a fuss; jolly lucky for us he isn't the one who gets ozard squared."

"Lucky!" echoed Jennings. "What about my bashing-up?"

"Are you frightened?" asked Darbishire.

"Well, just a bit. So'd you be; but I'm jolly well not going to tell Mr Carter."

Across the road was a sweet shop, and something about it rang a bell in Jennings' brain. Why should it appear vaguely familiar when he had never seen it before? "*S Valenti & Son*" was inscribed in red letters above the shop front, and a sign in the window informed the world that father and son specialised in the manufacture of genuine Brighton rock.

Jennings remembered. That must be the shop which Temple had visited when he foxed out last term. An idea buzzed in his brain, ticked over gently for a few seconds, then roared into action in top gear.

"I say, Darbi," he said, with growing excitement. "That sweet shop over there – "

"I don't feel much like sweets at the moment, thanks," said Darbishire.

"But that's the shop Temple went to when he foxed out."

"Well, you don't expect me to get excited over that, do you?"

"No, but I am," returned Jennings, as the idea assumed a practical shape. "Bang-on! I can see how to... Oh, blow! We haven't got any money; I wonder if Mr Carter'll let me have some more bank?"

When Mr Carter returned to say that the bus did not leave for an hour, he was a little puzzled about Jennings' insistence on buying Brighton rock; surely Jennings had plenty of sweets in his tuck-box, hadn't he?

"Yes, sir," replied Jennings earnestly; "but that won't do; it's got to be Brighton rock, and it's got to be in one of Valenti's bags with the name on."

Mr Carter looked searchingly at Jennings' anxious countenance.

"Is this rock very important?" he asked.

"Yes, sir. It's vital," Jennings assured him. "You know you said I'll have to settle this trouble by myself, sir? Well, I could do it if only I had some of that rock."

For a moment Mr Carter considered, and then he decided not to ask any questions. His instinct told him that if he were to wield the probe of official inquiry, he would agitate the molehill of friction into a mountain of trouble. This, he decided, was one of those cases which heal more quickly without interference.

He made further inroads on Jennings' bank and handed him a shilling.

"Coo, thank you, sir, thank you ever so!" Jennings hopped

41

on one leg in excited gratitude, and dashed across the road paying only the minimum of attention to his kerb drill.

Darbishire watched him, wondering what all the excitement was about. Then he looked at Mr Carter doubtfully.

"Are you going to take us back to school, sir?" he asked.

"That was the general idea," Mr Carter informed him.

"Oh," Darbishire said philosophically, "p'raps it won't be so bad, though. They say the first five years are the worst, don't they, sir?"

After Jennings' visit to Valenti's, Mr Carter took them to a restaurant, explaining that it would be bedtime before they got back to school.

Baked beans on toast restored their spirits and loosened their tongues, and Mr Carter was able to convince them that the rigours of school life were not nearly so bad as they had imagined.

"Venables, you dirty slacker, you haven't washed your feet!" said Atkinson.

The dormitory bell had rung some ten minutes before, and Temple, Atkinson and Venables had reached the gargling-gear-change stage of getting into bed.

They were rather puzzled at the absence of Jennings and Darbishire who had not appeared at tea, and seemed to have vanished from the face of the earth.

"Where on earth can those new characters have got to?" said Temple. "I haven't seen them since lunch."

"P'r'aps they're in the sick room," suggested Venables. "I say, Bod," he went on, as a thought struck him. "Weren't you going to bash one of them up before tea?"

"Gosh, yes! I forgot all about it," confessed the boxing champion. "Never mind, I'll do it tomorrow. No flowers by request; here lies Jennings; RIP."

"Who's talking about me?" demanded Jennings, sailing

into the dormitory as though he had just bought the place. He was followed by a smiling Darbishire.

"Golly! Where have you two been?" asked Atkinson. "The dorm bell went hours ago."

"And where were you at tea?" inquired Venables. "You missed some super-wizard muck. I had four helpings!"

Temple didn't like the self-satisfied expression on Jennings' face and said so.

"I know where they were," he said. "They've been hiding from me 'cos they funked getting bashed up."

"Good heavens, no!" said Jennings. "I never gave you a thought. I've had other things to think about. As a matter of fact, you chaps" – and he tried to make his voice sound casual – "as a matter of fact, Darbishire and I foxed out; we went into town on a bus."

A stunned silence followed this incredible statement. Temple was the first to recover.

"You – you never did!" he said in a hushed voice.

"Yes, didn't we, Darbi?" Jennings turned to his fellow conspirator for confirmation.

"That's right," said the conspirator. "We went out disguised like 'Dick Barton' – well, something like, anyway. It was super."

"And you cut tea as well!" breathed Atkinson admiringly. "Gosh! There'd have been the most frantic hoo-hah if you'd been caught."

"I couldn't have cared less," said Jennings nonchalantly. "I'm that sort, really, and Darbishire's a bit of a desperado in his way, too."

"Oh, you shouldn't say that," simpered the desperado modestly.

" 'Course he is," agreed Venables. "I think you're both wizard plucky and Bod isn't the only one after all. Good old Jen! You're smashing rare."

But Temple was not going to relinquish the victor's crown as easily as all that. "Don't you believe them," he broke in. "They're just making it up; I bet they can't prove it. Go on!" he jeered. "Just you prove it! I defy you to!"

Jennings produced the bag of rock with a flourish.

"Certainly," he said in the friendliest of voices. "Have a bit of Brighton rock, Bod; I got it at Valenti's."

Temple was so surprised that he couldn't speak, and Jennings passed the bag round with a lordly gesture that would have done credit to Mr Toad of Toad Hall.

"Sorry to pinch your idea, Bod," he went on, "but we improved on it rather, with our disguises. And it was just as well we had them, too" – he paused just long enough to produce the required effect – " 'cos Benedick got on the bus."

Again the remark was received in stupefied silence. Here, obviously, was some super-man!

"What?" gasped Venables when he had recovered from the shock.

"Oh, yes," said Jennings, as though evading the authorities was child's play. "But it was all right; we kept our heads, you see."

"Down," corrected Darbishire firmly.

"What's that, Darbishire?" asked Jennings.

"We kept our heads down," said Darbishire.

"And here we are to tell the tale," added Jennings, prudently leaving out quite a lot of the tale. "Have another bit of rock, Atki. It's genuine all right. See the name on the bag."

"Coo! Thanks, Jennings."

"Hand it round, Darbishire," Jennings went on. "Want another bit, Venables?"

"Coo! Thanks, Jennings," said Venables, his voice hushed with respectful awe. "I say, Jennings," he continued between mouthfuls, "look, you can share my basin if you like; you and Darbishire."

"No, have mine, Jennings," came from Atkinson, equally anxious to do homage to the famous. "Go on. And you and Darbishire can go first."

"Well, that's awfully decent of Atki," said Darbishire, basking in glory. "My father says that a generous impulse – "

"Don't be so modest, Darbishire," cut in Jennings. "No, I think we'll have Bod's basin."

Temple's throne tottered and fell.

"Well, yes; all right, Jennings," he heard himself say. "I'll wash first, then Darbishire, then you."

"Well, okay, then, Jennings."

"And no rot about bashing-up, eh, Bod."

Temple assured him that any mention of bashing-up had been in the nature of a friendly joke.

Jennings washed in a leisurely fashion and turned again to Temple.

"Oh, Bod," he said. "By the way, you don't mind my calling you Bod, do you, Bod?"

"No, that's all right, Jennings," returned Bod with an effort.

"Good. Well, I'm feeling a bit fagged out after foxing into town. You might clean this basin out for Darbishire, now I've finished washing my feet in it, will you?"

This was the crowning humiliation, but Temple's defences were shattered.

"Yes, Jennings… Okay, Jennings," he said.

4

Jennings Arrives Late

The crowd round the notice board parted to allow Mr Carter to pass through and pin the football teams on the board. The first practice of the term was due to start when afternoon preparation was over, and most of the new boys had been picked to play in "B" game; how they shaped in this would determine their football status for the next few weeks; the promising players would be promoted to "A" game, while the rabbits would find themselves relegated to the kick-and-rush contingent.

"Have you played much football, Jennings?" inquired Mr Carter.

"Yes, quite a lot, sir," Jennings replied. "I'm not at all bad, really."

"That's for us to decide," said Mr Carter, silencing the cry of " Swank" that went up on all sides. "And what about you, Darbishire?"

Darbishire had a profound distrust of ball games. His experience was somewhat limited as he had played football only once in his life, and what he chiefly remembered was that the ball travelled very fast and hurt when it hit you in the face and knocked your glasses off. This had happened early in the game, and he had removed his glasses for safety, with the result that his only other recollection was of being continually knocked off his feet by a seething mob who rushed around in pursuit of some apparently invisible object.

"I'm trying Jennings at centre-half," Mr Carter was saying. "Where would you like to play, Darbishire?"

Positions on the field meant nothing in Darbishire's life and this seemed a silly question. Surely there was only one place?

"I'd like to play on that field behind the chapel, please, sir," he replied, " 'cos it's next to the road, and I might be able to get some car numbers if they come close enough."

"What I mean is," explained Mr Carter, "which position do you want to play in? Forward? Half-back or where?"

Darbishire understood at last. "I think I'd like to be wicket-keeper, sir," he said, surprising himself by his ready command of sporting terms. There was a howl of laughter from the rest of the group who echoed the remark at the tops of their voices for the benefit of those out of earshot on the fringe of the circle. But Mr Carter kept a straight face.

"You'd better try outside-left, Darbishire," he said.

The bell rang for afternoon prep. It seemed a pity to have to waste the next forty minutes doing arithmetic, but the prospect of the game to follow gave Jennings sufficient strength to cope with the ordeal. He trooped off to his classroom and opened his books.

"Has anyone got my Arith. text-book?" demanded a certain Bromwich major, who occupied a place in the front row next to the master's desk. Nobody had, and Bromwich major bemoaned his fate.

"Oh, ozard egg!' he groaned. "Old Wilkie's taking prep and he'll blow up if I haven't got a book. Some ruinous oik's pinched it, I bet."

"You can have mine if you like, Bromo," said Jennings, "and I'll share with Darbishire."

"Coo, thanks," said Bromwich. "He'll never notice you two sharing at the back, but you must have a book if you sit where I do."

"Coming over by jet-propulsion," said Jennings. "Catch!"

Climbing steeply from a vertical take-off, the airborne volume sped on its way to the front row. But the Bromwich control tower was late with the landing-signal, and the book sailed through his clutching fingers and crash-landed on top of an uncorked bottle of ink that was reposing on the master's desk.

The master's desk was close to the classroom door. One entered the room; one turned sharp left; and there one was. And there, now, the overturned inkbottle was, with the ink flowing north and south over the desk, and gushing soddenly into tributaries and estuaries towards all the other points of the compass. Small lakes appeared at the lower contour levels, and shallow creeks to the north-west filled up as the work of irrigation spread.

"You clumsy goof," Bromwich shouted at his would-be benefactor, "you've spilt it all over the shop, and it's all down my exercise book, too. Gosh! There'll be a row about this; probably a number one priority hoo-hah; you see. Just you wait till Old Wilkie…"

He stopped abruptly for the time of waiting had already passed. As though attacked from without by a battering ram, the door hurtled open and Mr Wilkins was amongst those present. The door swung back on its hinges and crashed noisily into the corner of the master's desk, causing the overturned ink-bottle to roll gently over the top and come to rest in the middle of Bromwich major's exercise book.

Mr Wilkins' rapid glance took in the situation; the pirouetting ink-bottle, and the door still vibrating under the force of the impact. All the evidence pointed to his meteoric entrance as being the cause of the deluge.

"Good Lord!" he said appalled. "Did I do that? Heavens, yes! I must have done. Very clumsy! Sorry; sorry. Get some blotting paper someone, quick, and wipe it up. Tut-tut, tut-tut. Stupid of me!" He tut-tutted like a typewriter rattling off a line of print. "All over your book too, eh, Bromwich?" he went on. "Oh, well, can't be helped; no good crying over spilt milk."

Darbishire's hand went up at once.

"And you can put your hand down, Darbishire," said Mr Wilkins warmly. "I know just what you're going to say. Spilt 'ink,' not spilt 'milk.' Well, you needn't say it; I don't want to hear it. If I want to say milk I'll say milk, and I don't want anything about spilt ink from you, thanks very much."

"No, sir," said Darbishire humbly. "I was only going to say that there's a splodge of – er – milk on Bromwich major's nose, sir."

Mr Wilkins emitted a sound like a mediaeval fowling-piece being discharged at the Battle of Agincourt. "Corwumph," he barked.

The mess was mopped with blotting paper and blackboard duster, Mr Wilkins banning the use of off-white handkerchiefs that were freely offered and, in a highly explosive state of mind, he ordered work to begin.

Jennings was unable to concentrate on his arithmetic, as he was wondering whether he ought to confess that he was responsible for the spilt ink. He had not been asked to own up, of course, but that was merely due to Mr Wilkins jumping so hastily to the wrong conclusion. Would it be kind to disillusion him? It was easy for masters when they did something frightful, such as upsetting ink; they said they were sorry and everyone rushed to mop up. No one called them "clumsy goofs," and prophesied frantic "hoo-hahs" to follow.

The most peaceful solution was obviously to let sleeping

dogs lie, but Jennings' conscience kept throwing out a hint that it wasn't quite fair to let Mr Wilkins reproach himself for imaginary bottle-tilting. On the other hand, if there was going to be a hoo-hah, Jennings decided that he would make a few guarded inquiries about the consequences. He put up his hand.

"Sir," he said, as Mr Wilkins' raised eyebrow invited him to speak. "Sir, you know when you spilt the ink just now?"

"I do," said Mr Wilkins coldly.

"Well, sir, s'posing you hadn't."

Mr Wilkins raised the other eyebrow.

"No sense in supposing anything of the sort," he returned shortly. "If I spilt it, I spilt it; no point in making any bones about it. Get on with your prep."

"But, sir," persisted Jennings, "it's rather important. I know you thought you'd spilt it, and I know it looked as though you'd spilt it, but supposing you hadn't really spilt it after all, sir? What if it was just an optical illusion?"

Mr Wilkins began to look explosive. Nothing ignited his fuses so quickly as the idea that a boy was trying to rag him, and he interpreted Jennings' quest for knowledge as a deliberate attempt to be funny.

"Are you trying to be facetious, boy?" he demanded.

"No, honestly, sir," Jennings answered, shocked that his motive was being questioned.

"Well, don't talk nonsense, then. I'm not blind; I've got eyes in my head. I can see ink when it spills; I don't see things that aren't there."

"Not as a rule, no, sir, but what if you were led astray by appearances, sir? What if it were someone else who'd spilt it and not you; would it be all right for the someone else to say 'sorry' like you did, or as he wasn't you, would there be a row, sir?"

Mr Wilkins was sure by this time that the innocent

Jennings was trying to be funny. The boys knew how easily
Mr Wilkins came to the boil and they frequently put this
chemical experiment to the test in order to relieve the tedium
of a dull prep. And Mr Wilkins could not stand being
ragged.

"I – I – I – you – you – That's quite enough from you,
Jennings," he spluttered, the pinkish hue above his collar
flashing a danger signal.

"No, but honestly, sir," Jennings persisted rashly; and then
somebody laughed. It was this laugh, this open indication
that a rag was on the schedule of operations, that touched off
the fuse.

"Cor-wumph," he exploded, and this time it was as though
Dumas' trio of musketeers had let fly with a fusillade of
grapeshot from their blunderbusses.

"You can stay in during football," Jennings heard him say
as the reverberations died away and the dust settled. "And
now get on with your work; I don't want another sound out
of you."

Jennings could hardly believe his ears; he had had no
intention of being funny and he was not being punished for
spilling the ink, for indeed he had not been given a chance
to own up. Was it fair that truth should be muzzled, and his
honest attempts to shed light on this ink-stained episode
should meet with such a frightful fate? And he had been
looking forward to playing football more than he could say.
He returned to his sums with a rankling grievance against an
unfriendly world.

"Books away, quietly," boomed Mr Wilkins half an hour
later. "Quietly!" he yelled in a voice of thunder as some
unfortunate specimen in the front row let his desk lid fall
with a bang. "Right. Down to the changing-room and get
ready for football. All except Jennings, he stays here. Hurry
up. No running in the corridors. Anyone not changed in five

minutes doesn't play."

The form trooped out, scuffling sedately in their efforts to hurry without running. Jennings watched them unhappily; the thought of everyone, except him, enjoying themselves was too much; and the first game of the term, too! He had been going to show them how well he could play. He felt the tears welling up into his eyes as he turned his face away from the excited stream pouring out through the door.

Mr Wilkins advanced to Jennings' desk and glared balefully at the top of Jennings' bowed head. He would show new boys what happened if they tried to take a rise out of him. If the little beast was feeling pleased with himself he could stay there until he was laughing on the other side of his face. And then the faint plop of a tear dropping in the ink-well suggested that the little beast was feeling anything but pleased with himself. Mr Wilkins stared in surprise; perhaps he had been a bit harsh; perhaps... The truth was that Mr Wilkins' fiery manner concealed a kind heart. He was aware of this, and deliberately tried to stifle it by assuming righteous indignation and sending his temperature up to boiling point to ward off attacks on the kindliness of his nature. Only by this means, he felt, could he assert his authority and prevent the boys from taking advantage of him; but the old stagers knew that though Mr Wilkins' bark was brusque, his bite was largely bluff.

"What are you making that silly weeping noise for?" he demanded, steeling himself against the appeal for mercy that shone blearily through Jennings' tears.

"I don't know, sir," said Jennings damply.

"Suppose you want to be out playing football, eh?" Jennings nodded.

"Well, you've only got yourself to blame for that," said Mr Wilkins. "You should have thought of that before you tried to be funny."

"But I wasn't trying to be funny," urged Jennings. "I was only trying to tell you that you didn't spill the ink."

"Oh! I didn't spill the ink, didn't I?" said Mr Wilkins, switching on the current for his dangerous mood to warm up again. "I see; very funny. I didn't spill the ink, eh? Then since you know so much more about my actions than I do, do you mind telling me what I did do?"

"You didn't do anything, sir. You just came in and swung the door back."

"And I suppose the ink removed the cork from the bottle all by itself and then jumped out all over the desk?"

"No, sir."

"You surprise me. Who did spill it, then?"

"I did, sir."

Mr Wilkins stared at Jennings searchingly; the boy didn't look as though he was trying to be funny; perhaps this was some subtle trick designed for Mr Wilkins' humiliation and, if so, Mr Wilkins wanted some more data before he struck. "Go on," he said dangerously.

Jennings told all; the loan of the book; its near miss in the target area and its unhappy forced landing some two feet farther on; Mr Wilkins' cyclonic arrival and his error at jumping to hasty conclusions.

"And I was only going to tell you what really happened, sir, and you wouldn't let me and made me stay in," he finished, watching Mr Wilkins covertly to see how he took this fresh interpretation of the facts.

Mr Wilkins had been simmering gently during Jennings' recital; it was obvious that he was working up for something rather special. At last it came: with a bellow that could be heard by the boys in the changing-room below, he yelled aloud. Jennings shrank back in his desk to avoid damage by the blast, and then opened his eyes wide in amazement, for the bellow was not one of wrath, but one of mirth.

"Ha-ha-ha-ha!" roared Mr Wilkins, and the vibration set the pen rattling on Jennings' desk. "Ho-ho-ho-ho! That's the funniest thing I ever... Haw-haw-haw-haw!"

When Mr Wilkins laughed the matter could never be hushed up; his sense of humour was simple and he let it rip. Indeed, a crack in the staff-room ceiling was attributed, by Mr Carter, to Mr Wilkins' finding an unconsciously humorous sentence in a history essay that he had marked the previous term.

"Ha-ha-ha-ha!" The volume swelled like the diapason of an organ as Mr Wilkins, his countenance now a deep purple, saw the funny side. At last he recovered.

"Well," he boomed, wiping tears of mirth from his cheeks. "And there I was calling myself everything for being clumsy, and you wanting to own up and I wouldn't let you. Go on," he continued, "get downstairs and get changed; you'll still have time if you hurry."

"But what about the punishment, sir?" asked Jennings. He was still feeling a trifle cowed, for Mr Wilkins' humour was nearly as overpowering as Mr Wilkins' anger.

"What d'you mean – punishment?" returned Mr Wilkins. "There's no question of it, now I know you weren't trying to be funny on purpose."

"But for spilling the ink, sir."

"Oh!" said Mr Wilkins. "I see. Well, supposing it really had been me who spilt it, what sort of a punishment do you think I ought to have had?"

Jennings considered.

"I should say you ought to be let off with a caution," he volunteered.

"All right," said Mr Wilkins, "that suits me if it suits you; consider yourself cautioned; and now whip down to the changing-room before it's too late."

Jennings didn't need to be told twice. He shot out of the

classroom and, unmindful of school rules, scampered along the corridors to the changing-room. As he ran, he practised imaginary shots at goal. Wham! A beautiful corner kick, he decided, as the imaginary ball swerved in mid-air and, eluding the imaginary goalkeeper's frenzied fingers, crashed with a resounding thud into the net. How the imaginary crowd cheered! "Good old Jennings!" they yelled, clapping him on the back. "One-nil." He smiled with becoming modesty at a fire-extinguisher on the wall and prepared for the next phase. He decided on a penalty kick and, increasing his speed to the maximum as he rounded the corner to the changing-room, he let fly with his foot, making perfect contact with the ball. The imaginary aspect of the kick ended with sudden abruptness as his foot made perfect contact with an object that was certainly not a football. It was the Headmaster, and he received the full force of the penalty kick just below the knee-cap.

"Ough!" said the Headmaster in unacademic tones.

Martin Winthrop Barlow Pemberton-Oakes, Esq, MA (Oxon), Headmaster, was not normally a devotee of the ballet but, on this occasion, he executed a number of *pas de chats* and *grands jetés* that would have done credit to a prima ballerina. When the pain had abated somewhat, he placed his injured leg gently back on the ground and looked down to ascertain the cause of the trouble.

"I'm terribly sorry, sir," said Jennings. "I didn't know you were coming round the corner."

"This is a school," began the Headmaster, "and not a bear garden. It has rules for the benefit of people who wish to turn corners without being kicked on the knee-cap. If, therefore, I make a rule that no boy shall run in the corridors, I am at a loss to understand why my instructions are disregarded, and I find you running to the public danger and committing crimes of assault and battery."

"No, sir," said Jennings.

The Headmaster was not used to having odd remarks interpolated into his speeches.

"No, sir? What do you mean, 'No, sir?' Are you disagreeing with what I said?" he demanded in the iciest of head-magisterial tones.

"No, sir. I mean, no, I didn't suppose you could understand – er – what you said, sir. I was agreeing with you, really, sir."

"Kindly note, Jennings, that when I make a remark that is not a question, neither comment nor answer is required."

"Yes, sir – er – I mean – no comment," said Jennings hastily.

"You will return to your classroom, Jennings, and meditate upon the fate that awaits small boys who run in corridors. Why on earth you can't behave like a civilised human being is beyond me!"

Jennings was not sure whether this one required an answer, or was another of those "no comments." The Headmaster had certainly asked why, but Jennings decided that it might be rash to embark upon a lengthy explanation.

The teams had finished changing for games and were streaming out on to the field as Jennings returned to his classroom. He watched them gloomily from the window. This was the end; no football today and, if he went on like this, there probably wouldn't be any, ever.

He was still thinking bitter thoughts three minutes later when he saw the Headmaster standing in the doorway.

"Well, Jennings, have you meditated upon your misdeeds?" His knee-cap was hurting less now and he felt more inclined to be lenient to a new boy, who perhaps had not had enough time to become used to school life.

"Yes, sir," replied Jennings.

"In that case you may once more proceed to the changing-room, this time at a walking pace."

Jennings' first impulse was to say, "Coo, thanks, sir," but decided that it might be interpreted as a comment upon the Headmaster's judgment, so he said nothing.

"Well," said the Headmaster, "haven't you anything to say?"

"Yes, sir. Thanks very much, sir."

Masters were funny, Jennings thought, as he walked sedately to the changing-room. One minute they ticked you off for answering and the next they ticked you off because you didn't. Golly, but he would have to hurry if he wanted to play football; the game had started hours ago, and, if he wasn't there soon, he wouldn't be allowed to play.

There wasn't time to change properly and take everything off, so he removed his jacket and put his white sweater on instead. He wasted precious seconds trying to pull his football shorts over the trousers he was already wearing, but they were too tight, so he rolled up his trouser legs a couple of inches and pulled his voluminous white sweater down till it reached nearly to his knees and gave no sign of what he was wearing underneath. Socks were easier; the second pair went over the top of the first without much difficulty and he had only to put his football boots on and he would be ready. Gosh, it must be nearly half-time; everyone else had gone out ages ago!

Not quite everyone, though, for as he made a dive for his football boots, he saw Darbishire sitting on the floor in front of the boot-lockers.

"What on earth are you doing here, Darbi?" he demanded.

"It's these stupid boots," replied Darbishire. "My mother tied them together by the laces when she packed them, so's I wouldn't lose one without the other – not that I wanted to lose both" – he went on in case his meaning should not be quite clear – "but she thought there'd be more chance of neither getting lost if – "

Jennings cut short the explanation.

"Well, you haven't lost them, so why don't you put them on?"

"I can't undo the knot," said Darbishire sadly. "I've been tugging at it for about twenty minutes, and the harder I tug, the tighter the knot gets."

"Gosh! Yes, you have got it into a mess," agreed Jennings, inspecting the four lace ends tied inextricably together. "I shouldn't think anyone could undo that, now, but you'll just have to put them on and put up with it. There'll be an awful how-d'you-do if you don't turn up, and you don't want that, do you?"

"No, I don't want a 'how-d'you-do,'" said Darbishire, solemnly eyeing the laces. "What I really want is a 'how-d'you-undo.'"

Darbishire thought that his prowess as a footballer would be severely handicapped if he had to play with both feet tied together, but as this seemed preferable to the official wrath that his absenteeism would incur, he put on his boots and shuffled to the door. The tied laces permitted him to take a step of about ten inches and, assisted by Jennings, he proceeded in an ungainly shamble to the football field. They looked a queer pair, as Jennings' bulk was increased by his day clothes beneath his sweater, and as this capacious garment was pulled down almost to his knees, it appeared as though he had absentmindedly forgotten to wear any trousers.

Mr Carter was taking the game and decided not to waste any more time in demanding explanations of their late arrival.

"I've put Brown at centre-half as you weren't here, Jennings," he said. "You'd better play – let me see – what are we short of?"

They were standing near the goal and the goalkeeper, one Paterson, immediately chipped in.

"Can I come out of goal, sir? I'm getting super cold standing about and Jennings has got a sweater and goalkeepers always wear sweaters, sir, it says so in the Laws of the game, honestly, sir, and as I haven't got a sweater, sir," he went on without pausing for breath, "I'm really breaking the rules, and Jennings ought to be jolly good in goal with a super sweater like that, oughtn't he, sir?"

As Paterson looked chilly, Mr Carter despatched him to the forward line and sent Jennings to keep goal.

"And where did I say you were to play, Darbishire?" he asked.

"You said I was to be left out, sir," replied Darbishire.

"Left out of what?"

"I don't know out of what, sir; just left outside somewhere."

"Yes, I remember," said Mr Carter, as light dawned. "Outside-left, not left outside."

The game was fast and furious and Mr Carter was too busy to notice Darbishire's crippling progress to the left wing. It took him some time and much inquiry to get there, but finally he reached a spot near the touch-line where he was out of the hurly-burly and there he stood, somewhat awkwardly, at ease.

Jennings' goal was hard pressed by the opposing forwards and after saving eight shots in four minutes – three good saves and five lucky ones – he began to feel uncomfortably warm, but to remedy his over-dressed condition would have been asking for trouble. He mopped his brow and saw that the opposing forwards were launching yet another attack. The ball came lolloping towards him – an easy shot to save – and he gathered it into his hands without difficulty, but before he could clear it to his forwards he was hemmed in on three sides by his determined opponents. What could he do?

Washbrooke major was winding up the whole of his six stone seven pounds for a tremendous barge which would have knocked Jennings and the ball far over the goal line. The goal-posts were not fitted with nets, so Jennings decided to retreat and, still clasping the ball, he stepped back over his own goal line, skipped nimbly round the post and punted the ball up the field. The whistle blew.

"Goal," said Mr Carter.

"But, sir, it can't be," argued Jennings, " 'cos I saved it; I caught it before it crossed the line."

"But you took it over the line when you dodged round the post," Mr Carter explained.

"Oh, but that was just to get away from Washbrooke; I'd saved it hours before that."

Mr Carter looked more closely at the perspiring goalkeeper.

"What are you wearing?" he demanded, and proceeded to investigate. "Vest, shirt, pullover, tie, underpants, braces, day trousers – with bulging pockets – boots, two pairs of socks and an outsize sweater," he reeled off. "Are you sure you wouldn't like your overcoat as well?"

Jennings' explanation was unavailing, and for the third time that afternoon he headed towards the changing-room as Mr Carter restarted the game.

Darbishire rather liked playing outside-left. It was peaceful, he decided; the frantic battles of the midfield seemed remote, and it was unlikely that anyone would disturb the serene stillness by kicking the ball to this quiet backwater near the touch line.

There were some wild flowers growing on the bank a few yards away and he would have liked to wander off and pick them, but for the distressing handicap around his ankles. Never mind, he would pretend that he was a prisoner in a chain gang and was condemned to spend ten years with his feet securely... The train of thought jolted to a sudden halt. The worst was about to happen; some ill-advised athlete had sent a pass out to the left wing and the ball was coming straight at Darbishire. Now what was it that one was supposed to do? Oh, yes, kick the ball; the direction didn't matter, the main thing being to boot the beastly thing as far away as possible and hope that it didn't come back.

"Go on, Darbishire," called his captain. "Kick!"

It would be stretching the facts to say that Darbishire kicked the ball but the spirit was willing even though the flesh was weak and held together at the ankles by bootlaces. He drew his right foot back the full ten inches that the latitude of his laces allowed and swung his boot forward as hard as he could. The impetus of the forward swing dragged the other foot with it; up into the air went both feet, and Darbishire fell flat on his back while the ball rolled harmlessly over the touch-line.

The boys who assisted Darbishire to his feet were almost helpless with laughter.

"What happened, Darbishire?" they asked. "Did you have a stroke?"

"Oh, no, nothing so serious," Darbishire assured them. "It's merely a sort of temporary disability that I'm suffering from."

Mr Carter took one look at the inextricable knots, and cut the temporary disability with his penknife. Two minutes later, as he blew his whistle to end the game, Jennings arrived, correctly changed and anxious for the fray.

5

The Bells Go Down

"I don't think I shall ever get into the First Eleven," said Darbishire some days later; "not even if I tried ever so."

"Well, I'm jolly well going to try and get in," said Jennings. "I'm going to practise like anything, and I dare say if I go on getting better and better I shall play for England one day. Not for a few years yet, of course," he amended.

Jennings was certainly a promising player, though too erratic to be sure of a place in the Eleven, and he had felt a tinge of disappointment the previous Saturday when the team to play Bracebridge School had been posted and his name was not included. It was an "away" match, too, which was much more exciting as it involved a journey by motor coach, and the prospects of a large tea.

"You ought to take some interest in football, Darbishire, 'cos everyone'll think you're the most radio-active sissy if you don't."

"I know what, then," said Darbishire. "I'll be a sports reporter like they have in the newspapers, and I'll report the matches for the school magazine. Then everybody'll read my column and see what I've got to say, and I might even write some hints on how to improve your play like the Internationals do, and that'd make me spivish important in football circles, wouldn't it?"

"M'yes, so long you only told people what to do and didn't try to give a demonstration."

The two boys were waiting for choir practice to begin. This consisted chiefly of practising sea shanties for the end of term concert, and was a popular after-lunch event because Mr Wilkins was in charge.

Mr Wilkins did not teach music, as he was not considered sufficiently accomplished for so important an undertaking, but he could batter his way through "Shenandoah" and "A Drunken Sailor" on the piano, and the Headmaster considered that if Mr Wilkins' voice was good for anything at all, it was good enough for sea-shanties.

Mr Wilkins entered the Assembly Hall and marched towards the piano.

"Page forty-four, *Fire Down Below*," he announced in a voice which suggested that he was trying to broadcast to the nation without using a microphone. He struck a few chords tentatively.

"Ooh, sir!" winced Nuttall, who had a keen ear for harmony.

"What's the matter?" demanded Mr Wilkins, pausing in mid-discord.

"Wrong note, sir. Right out of the target area, sir."

"Oh, I don't know," replied Mr Wilkins. "It wasn't too bad for a near miss."

He pressed on. He did not claim to be a good pianist, and if at times he let not his right hand know what his left hand did, he got over this by drowning the piano altogether with his stentorian baritone.

The words and something vaguely resembling the tune of *Fire Down Below* were wafted by the breeze to the ears of Mr Carter and the Headmaster as they crossed the quad.

"I've had another letter from Mr Jennings," the Headmaster was saying. "Apparently he can't make much sense of the boy's weekly letter home, and he's still rather concerned to know how he's fitting in with school life."

The Headmaster prided himself on knowing everything about the boys in his care, and regretted that so far he had not had time to make a close examination of Jennings and his characteristics. All he knew was that the boy displayed a tendency to kick people on the knee-cap, and that was hardly sufficient evidence on which to form a judgment. Mr Jennings' obvious concern seemed to indicate that his son was one of those delicate, highly-strung boys.

Mr Carter did not agree; he thought Jennings was about as highly strung as a shrimping net and as delicate as a bulldozer.

"He's like a cork in the water," he explained, "you can push him under, but the next moment he's bobbing about on the top again."

The Headmaster decided to watch Jennings closely.

"What on earth is that extraordinary noise coming from the Assembly Hall, Carter?" he asked, as Fire Down Below started up again after a short break for resting the lungs.

They were just outside the windows by this time and they had to raise their voices to make themselves heard,

"It's Wilkins, sir. He's holding a choir practice."

"Speak up; I can't hear," said the Headmaster.

"Wilkins – choir practice," repeated Mr Carter.

"Fire practice?" said the Headmaster in surprise. "But surely he doesn't imagine that singing *Fire Down Below* would be the slightest use in extinguishing a conflagration?"

"No, not 'fire' practice; 'choir' practice."

"Ah yes, of course. That reminds me," the Headmaster went on, his mind jumping from one topic to the other with the agility of a mountain goat, "we ought to have one this afternoon; we haven't had one for a long time."

Mr Carter was a few moves behind in these mental

gymnastics.

"But they're having one now, sir," he insisted. "I just told you; the choir are practising for the concert."

"No, no, no, Carter; I'm talking about 'fire' practice, not 'choir' practice; you mentioned it yourself. Now, when Wilkins has finished tuning the piano and making those extraordinary vocal contortions, we'll send the boys up to their dormitories and let them come down on the 'Pennetra' fire-escape."

The rules governing an outbreak of fire were prominently displayed in all dormitories, and practices were held at intervals. All boys stood quietly by their beds; a gong was sounded and when various formalities had been attended to, they would proceed down the main staircase in an orderly file. The alternative was descent by the Escape. This consisted of a steel box screwed to the window frame and containing a roll of cable with a sling on the end. Placing the sling under the armpits, one lowered oneself into space from the window-sill, and descended gently to the ground as the life-line was automatically paid out from above. It was a very popular undertaking, but as a rule it was only used under the supervision of the masters.

"No," continued the Headmaster. "We'll go one better than that; we won't tell them to use the Escape. We'll just say that the staircase is impassable and let them use their initiative."

It was the Headmaster's custom to test the boys' intelligence and powers of leadership by making one of them responsible for discovering an imaginary fire and seeing how he reacted to the ensuing emergencies.

As soon as Mr Wilkins had finished, the Headmaster strode into the Assembly Hall and addressed the school.

"Now that we've finished with *Fire Down Below*," he began, "we're going to start on 'fire up above.' Ha-ha-ha! Oh!"

Vacant expressions on seventy-nine faces indicated that his little joke had fallen flat, so he proceeded to explain.

"We are going to assume an outbreak of fire on the top landing outside Dormitory Four; now what is the first thing to do?"

Seventy-eight hands went up and the Headmaster noted that the absentee hand belonged to Jennings.

"Well Darbishire? Perhaps you can tell me."

"You use your intelligence, sir," said Darbishire, paraphrasing Fire Rule No. 1. "And if you can't think of anything intelligent, you call one of the masters and do what he says instead."

"M'yes," said the Headmaster, not knowing how to take this remark. "But supposing that no master is available?"

Again seventy-eight hands shot up, but Jennings was at Lord's, where he had just scored a century against the Australians in the most exciting Test match that had been seen for years.

The Headmaster decided that now would be the time to test the boy's initiative; he would put him in charge of the fire drill and see what happened.

"Let us assume," he continued, "that instead of being half-past two in the afternoon it is half-past two in the morning, and a boy in Dormitory Four – let us say Jennings, for example – awakens from sleep."

The mention of his name recalled Jennings from Lord's, where he had just put himself on to bowl at the pavilion end. He came to with a start.

"I beg your pardon, sir?" he said.

"I said, Jennings awakens from sleep," repeated the Headmaster; "but judging from your appearance while I have been speaking, I was beginning to think you had gone into a state of hibernation for the winter. I trust that is not so?"

"I don't know, sir," replied Jennings. "I don't know what

hiber – what you said – means, sir."

"It applies to such creatures as toads, moles, bats and, apparently, to some small boys," explained the Headmaster; "derived from the Latin word *hiberna* meaning winter – it means – well, think, boy, think."

Jennnings thought hard, but the atmosphere of Lord's still hung about him.

"Well, Jennings, what does a bat do in the winter?"

"It – er – it splits if you don't oil it, sir," he said.

The Headmaster took the blow without flinching and explained the rules of the drill. Jennings, waking from slumber in the middle of the night, was to find a hypothetical fire; he was to assume that no master was at hand and, if his imagination stretched so far, that the stairs had fallen in. Could he cope with such a situation?

Jennings thought he could, but suggested that, if they had to assume the fire, and the fallen staircase was but a figment of the imagination, surely logic demanded that they could pretend to put on imaginary asbestos suits, or jump into a supposed sheet that they could pretend was being held below.

"Certainly not," said the Headmaster. "Having imagined the circumstances, everything else will be done exactly as though a conflagration had actually occurred. Exactly – do you understand? The rules for fire drill will be obeyed to the letter."

"Yes, sir, but supposing – "

"There will be no supposing. This is a test of your initiative, Jennings. I shall give you a few minutes to look over the rules and think out your plan of action; after that, you will sound the gong and I shall await the result with interest."

As soon as they were in the dormitory, Jennings took charge.

"Now, all put your pyjamas on," he said; "we're supposed to be hibernating to start with, and when you wake up the room's full of smoke."

"Coo, yes," agreed Darbishire. "And I vote we soak our towels in the wash basins and tie them over our noses and crawl round and round the floor where the air's purer."

"Coo, yes, spiv on," said Atkinson. "We could pretend we're looking for the way out, but the smoke's so thick, we keep crawling past the door without seeing it."

The list of fire drill instructions was discovered rammed in the keyhole of the door. Venables explained that a "super-hairy" breeze whistled through the keyhole and, sleeping where he did, a bung was necessary to exclude the draught.

"Get it out, then," said Jennings. "We'll have to see what to do."

"I know one thing it says," put in Temple, as Venables attacked the keyhole with his penknife, "we have to close all doors and windows; something to do with the draught."

"That's crackers," returned Jennings. "How can we get out if all the doors are closed, and who's going to worry about being in a draught, anyway, if the place is on fire?"

This led to a brief argument. One school of thought contended that doors and windows should be opened, while the rival philosophy held that doors should be opened to allow the exit of all personnel, while windows should be closed to prevent the fire from going out.

"But we want the fire to go out, don't we?" said Darbishire.

"Not out of the windows, we don't," replied Jennings. "No, I think it's open doors to make the flames burn up nice and bright, so's the firemen can see where the fire is."

The argument was ended by Venables producing the screwed-up copy of the rules from the keyhole.

"It says here," he announced, "that first of all we've got to use our initiative."

"I'd much rather use the staircase," said Jennings. "Here, let's have a look." And, taking the paper from Venables, he read out: "*Any boy discovering an outbreak of fire at night will sound the alarm gong and inform Mr Carter, who will telephone for the fire brigade.*"

"Yes, but the Head said we were to do it without Mr Carter." objected Darbishire. "What's it say about that?"

"*If no master is available*," continued Jennings, "*boys must use*... Something. I can't read it."

"Staircase?" suggested Darbishire.

"No, 'initiative,' that's it. *Boys will keep calm and* – Blah, blah, blah." He skipped the next few paragraphs as they looked dull. "And there's a bit at the end that says the boy finding the fire will be Wally."

"Wally?" echoed Temple. "But that's crazy; we haven't got anyone called Wally."

"That's what it says, anyway."

Temple snatched the paper from Jennings and read: "*The boy who discovers the fire will be*... Oh, you are a fool, Jennings, that's not 'Wally,' that's 'wholly'. You're to be wholly concerned with seeing that everyone – "

"Well, let's get cracking, anyway," said Jennings. "You chaps put your pyjamas on and start opening and closing all the doors and windows."

Darbishire was allowed to go out on to the landing with Jennings as "*assistant gong-biffer*," and there he proceeded to warn his friend how careful one had to be with fire, as witness the minor calamity that had befallen the Darbishire household last holidays.

"My father was making a piece of toast on the gas stove in the kitchen," he recounted in dramatic tones, "and suddenly it caught alight, and before he knew where he was, there was a mighty 'swoosh' and – "

"Why didn't he know where he was?" demanded Jennings.

"He did. He was making a piece of toast in the kitchen."

"But you said it went 'swoosh' before he knew where he was," objected Jennings. "And if he was in the kitchen all the time, he must have known, unless he was suffering from loss of memory."

"Oh, don't be such a hairy ruin," said Darbishire. "Hadn't we better get this fire started?"

Jennings gave the matter some thought. Everything had to be done as though the fire were real, and not merely a Headmaster's whimsical notion of the best way to spend a half-holiday.

In an actual outbreak, Mr Carter would telephone for the fire brigade, but one of the hazards of the exercise was that Jennings' own initiative must take the place of help from a grown-up source. Surely, then, the Headmaster expected him to summon the necessary assistance; that was what he must have meant when he had demolished the staircase with a wave of his hand; obviously a turntable ladder alone could save them from an inflammable fate. Probably the Headmaster had already warned the fire brigade and they were even now standing by with engines ticking over, waiting for the call to action. He must not fail in this test of initiative.

But Darbishire was appalled at so bold a plan.

"Couldn't you just pretend?" he suggested.

"Huh! You heard what he said when I suggested pretending to wear asbestos suits," Jennings scathed back at him. "I bet the first thing he says is, 'Have you given the jolly old hose squirters a tinkle on the blower?'"

"He doesn't talk like that," objected Darbishire. "And s'posing he hasn't – the firemen'll be ever so cross; s'posing they're just going to have their tea and s'posing it's something wizard – like baked beans on toast – it'd be all spoilt by the time they got back."

"How d'you know they have baked beans for tea at fire stations?"

"I don't, only – "

"Well, then, that proves it," said Jennings conclusively. "The trouble with you, Darbishire, is you've got no finish. Besides, how else can we get out if we can't go down the stairs?"

The logic of this argument swayed Darbishire. Neither he nor Jennings thought of the Escape. Never having used it, they vaguely imagined that the metal contraption on the window-sill was for ornamental purposes, or at best, some labour-saving device connected with polishing the linoleum. The other members of the dormitory had been instructed in the correct use of the apparatus in the past and might have guessed the Headmaster's intention, but they, alas, remained in ignorance of Jennings' plan of campaign.

Darbishire held the gong steady and Jennings beat it with gusto. While the echoes were still resounding throughout the building, windows opened in the dormitories; life lines whirred into action and an orderly evacuation began in all dormitories except one; for in No. 4 on the top storey, the boys, swathed in damp towels, were crawling round and round the floor on their hands and knees according to instructions.

Jennings sped along to Mr Carter's room. Fortunately this was on the top floor, so the difficulty of bridging the gulf left by the disappearing staircase did not arise. He tapped on the door; no answer. The room, as expected, was empty.

Jennings made for the telephone on the desk. What should he say? Well, he'd just ask them if they'd mind sending the turntable ladder as the stairs had fallen in and there were some people to be rescued on the top floor.

The clock on Mr Carter's desk stood at ten minutes to

three as Jennings lifted the receiver from its rest.

"Fire station, please," he said importantly.

Dunhambury Fire Station was situated in centre of the town some five miles from Linbury Court. It was normally a smart and efficient station, particularly when Leading Fireman Cuppling was on duty. To him it was a matter of pride that branch-pipes glistened and stand-pipes shone; that hose was rolled with geometrical neatness, and that mechanical equipment went like clockwork.

Judge then, of the leading fireman's horror and dismay when at half-past two he went to inspect the appliance to which he had been assigned for the rest of the day. The board on which the crews and available appliances were marked had given no hint of the rude shock that awaited him. "Turntable ladder," read the board. "In charge: Leading Fireman Cuppling. Crew: Fireman Long and Fireman Short."

And the turntable, when the leading fireman reached it, was not upholding the traditions for spick-and-span smartness on which the station prided itself.

"Well, darn my socks!" he murmured, recoiling in distaste from the monstrosity before him. Tarnished brass, dirty wet hose, green slime on the suction-basket and mud on wings and windscreen met his astonished gaze. Never had he seen such an untidy vehicle. The crew's helmets and boots lay inextricably tangled amongst a welter of hose ramps, breeching-pieces and petrol cans, and the casual observer, might have thought that the turntable had just finished coping with an outbreak of fire in a rubbish dump.

But this was not so. Life in the neighbourhood of Dunhambury was so devoid of excitement, that nothing but the spontaneous combustion of a haystack, or the accidental firing of a soot-filled chimney, ever disturbed the orderly routine of the fire station. And haystacks and chimneys were beneath the dignity of the turntable ladder. It was a magnificent appliance and, in the expert hands of Leading Fireman Cuppling, the hundred-foot ladder would rear up towards the sky, shooting forward and sideways, with the controlled ease of a sea-serpent stretching its flexible neck.

The pity of it was that such an intricate piece of machinery should be used only for rescuing stray cats from the church roof and cleaning the top storey windows at the fire station; but the type of fire needed to show off its paces was rare in that rural Sussex countryside.

Leading Fireman Cuppling blinked in dismay at the unkempt appearance of his pride and joy, and his expression was grim as he went in search of his crew.

Fireman Long and Fireman Short were admirable and intrepid fire-fighters, but they had a habit of retiring to some out of the way spot when the more unpleasant routine jobs had to be attended to.

Cuppling ran them to earth in the fire-tower where, comfortably seated on a pile of hose, they were mechanically stroking a stand-pipe with a polishing cloth in the intervals of filling in their football coupons.

"Oh, hallo, Archie. Come to give us a hand?" Fireman Long, better known as Lofty, greeted his superior with a heartiness that was meant to disarm suspicion, while Fireman Short tactfully concealed the coupons in his cap.

"Not so much of the 'Archie,'" returned the Leading Fireman in official tones. "It's Leading Fireman Cuppling to you when I'm on duty, and don't you forget it. And what do you two think you're doing, hiding yourselves away like this?"

"Hiding?" echoed Fireman Long in pained accents. "Tut-tut, as though we would! Shorty and me are doing a bit of brass polishing. Got this stand-pipe up nice and bright, haven't we?"

"It doesn't take two of you to clean one stand-pipe."

"Oh, yes, it does," Lofty assured him. "You see, Shorty breathes on it while I give it the old how-d'you-do with the cloth. Go on, Shorty," he added to his friend. "Get breathing."

Fireman Short obeyed by exhaling stertorously.

"Hurr-hurr-hurr." He emptied his lungs and paused for breath.

"Saves wasting brass polish, see?" explained Lofty.

"That's not funny," said Archie Cuppling. "And I seem to remember that's the same stand-pipe you were cleaning yesterday."

"That's right, Archie – er – Leading Fireman Cuppling, I mean," replied Lofty. "Yesterday it was my turn to breathe while Shorty polished, see? So now it's only fair to..."

The Leading Fireman cut short this plausible explanation and demanded to know why the turntable ladder was so dirty and untidy. He had been out all morning testing hydrants, but Long and Short had been posted to the turntable all day and could be held responsible for its condition.

The story was soon told. Early that morning they had been instructed to take the appliance to the river to test the pinup and the hose. The river was tidal at Dunhambury and as the tide was low, they had had to drive on to the mud flats in order to get near the water. There the worst had happened; the wheels had stuck in the mud, and in their efforts to release them, they had plastered themselves, and everything with which they had come in contact, with the fertile silt of the river Dun. A heavy shower of rain had not improved matters, but eventually the machine was freed; the pump was tested, the hose was found to withstand the required pressure per square inch, and Lofty and Shorty had returned to restore their jaded tissues with cups of tea and cheese sandwiches.

"But darn my socks!" expostulated the Leading Fireman when the recital was finished. "All this happened this morning. It's twenty to three and you haven't done a thing about cleaning it. You'd no business to have knocked off for dinner till you'd squared everything up. Come on, we're going to start work."

"Work?" echoed Fireman Short faintly. "What, only us three? You ought to have four men on a turntable, you know."

"Well, you can do the work of two," was all the sympathy he got from his Leading Fireman, who then proceeded to outline his plans for a pleasant Wednesday afternoon. "We'll have every piece of equipment stripped off and cleaned, and all that wet hose scrubbed and replaced." He glowed with enthusiasm for the job on hand and, bursting with vitality, led the way to the appliance with his fingers itching to get to work.

Lofty and Shorty followed at a more dignified pace.

"Pity he's rumbled us," said Lofty. "Nice and warm in the tower it was, too."

"Ah! What about our football pools?" put in Shorty. "If we lose fifty thousand quid whose fault will it be? Leading Fireman Cuppling's, that's whose, if Bolton Wanderers beat Charlton, which they've got a good chance of, and we miss the post on account of changing the hose an' all."

"Come on," shouted the Leading Fireman. "You don't get paid good money to hang about nattering all day. Everything off, now," he ordered; "branches, nozzles, stand-pipes, suction, breeching-pieces, wrenches – all of it."

Metallic clangs and dull thuds, accompanied by gruntings and blowings, announced that the crew were battling with the equipment.

Archie Cuppling set the pace and worked like a dynamo,

ANTHONY BUCKERIDGE

which reminded Lofty that it was time he had a look at the
carburettor. He was a good mechanic and felt that, when the
work on fire stations became more than usually unpleasant,
it was the privilege of all good mechanics to retire from the
hurly-burly and devote themselves to some quiet and
contemplative task such as inspecting plugs and testing
leads. It was a foolproof way of avoiding the miseries of hose
scrubbing, for no one could deny the importance of a well-
tuned engine. But today the ruse was unsuccessful.

"Come on out of it," called Cuppling, prodding him ever
so gently from behind with a ceiling hook. "You can mess
about under the bonnet when we've got all this hose
scrubbed."

The good mechanic's feelings were outraged.

"Now, look here, Archie," he said, "be reasonable. If I've
got to drive this perishing bus, I've got a right to check the
engine."

"I've heard that one before," replied his superior, struggling
to carry a thirty-foot ladder unaided. "As soon as there's any
heavy work going you lie flat on your back and make out
you've got to polish the exhaust pipe." With a superhuman
effort he heaved the ladder on to the *Self-Propelled*, and sped
back to the turntable.

"But the jet's choked in the carburettor," Lofty complained.
"We kept stalling all the way up from the river. If I don't get
it cleaned, we'll be up a gum tree if we have to turn out to a
job."

This was true; the carburettor had given trouble that
morning, but Fireman Long had cried "Wolf" so often that
Archie Cuppling took no notice and, in spite of his protests,
Lofty was ordered to assist with the work of unloading.

By now the floor in the vicinity of the turntable was piled
high with equipment, and Archie ordered all the dirty hose
to be taken out into the yard.

76

"Cor! Blow me!" grumbled Shorty. "We aren't 'arf 'aving a spring clean! What'll I do with our boots; there's no room for 'em here?"

"Take them over there by the *Self-Propelled*," came the answer. "We'll have them washed before we put them back."

Shorty ambled across the room and dumped his load next to some dozen pairs of wellington boots which belonged to the other crews. A thought struck him.

"Here," he said, "hadn't you better tell the control room as this turntable ladder isn't available? S'pose we got a fire call?"

It was then that Leading Fireman Cuppling made his big mistake.

"Don't you worry about that," he said. "The turntable hasn't been sent to a fire for three years, so I don't think that having the kit off for a quarter of an hour is going to be much of a risk." And with demoniacal energy that made Fireman Short feel quite faint, he picked up three lengths of wet hose and trotted briskly into the yard.

Soon the appliance had been stripped of all its equipment. Leading Fireman Cuppling, bubbling over with zest and vitality, made short work of the fertile silt of the river Dun, while sounds of splashings from the yard outside announced that Firemen Long and Short, having run out the dirty hose, were busily engaged in scrubbing it. *Busily engaged?* That, perhaps, is an exaggeration; but they were sluicing water in all directions, in the time-honoured belief that what was wet, was clean.

At nine minutes to three precisely, the bells "went down." With a clanging that woke the echoes for acres around, the alarm bells shrilled out their urgent message in tones to rouse the dead.

Fireman Long paused in the act of rolling a cigarette.

"Fire-call," he said, stating the obvious.

"We shan't be wanted, anyway," said Fireman Short, resting heavily on the handle of his broom. It was taken for granted at Dunhambury that the turntable ladder would never be needed at local fires, and that the crew enjoyed a holiday from fire fighting so long they were posted to this particular vehicle; therefore, they did not hurry, but watched with a leisurely interest as firemen came running from all quarters at the summons of the alarm. Bodies slid down poles, heads popped up through trapdoors, and everywhere legs were running, feet were jumping into boots, and arms waved themselves into tunics.

The other appliances were manned and had their engines running when Lofty and Shorty sauntered into the appliance room. A second later an agonised figure shot out of the control room. It was Leading Fireman Archie Cuppling, and his face was contorted by every emotion from alarm to despondency.

"Turntable ladder!" he shouted, as he raced down the station. "Quick! Quick! It's a turn-out!"

The news was incredible, but the message he bore in his hand confirmed these strange tidings. "Linbury Court School," it said. "Persons believed trapped third floor. TL required for rescue."

"We can't turn out to no fire with our kit all over the shop like a blinking jumble sale," gasped Shorty. "What are we going to do?"

"Bung it all back again, quick," yelled his Leading Fireman. "Hurry up! Hurry up! Come on, you fellows, give us a hand," he called to the other crews who were now emerging from their appliances and de-booting themselves. "And get the engine started Lofty, quick. Oh, darn my socks!" he groaned to himself as the alarm bell ceased ringing. "We've wasted a minute already!"

A slow turn-out to a fire call is the most serious of crimes, and Archie Cuppling alternately boiled with rage and froze with shame at his own lack of foresight, as he led the work of piling on the equipment.

"Faster! Faster!" he encouraged them. "Chuck it on anywhere for now; we'll sort it out when we get there. But, for goodness' sake, get a move on!"

The entire station personnel hurried as they had never hurried before. They ran pell-mell with stand-pipes; they ran helter-skelter with branch holders; they ran full tilt with petrol cans, and they ran posthaste with the suction hose. But Leading Fireman Cuppling eclipsed them all in the ferocity of his attack upon the job in hand. He pell-melled; he helter-skeltered; he full-tilted, and he post-hastened until, some two minutes later, most of the apparatus was aboard.

Lofty was in the driver's seat with his hand on the self-starter, but the engine refused to co-operate.

"She won't have it," he shouted to no one in particular. "It's that there choked carburettor."

"What's that?" shouted Archie above the clatter of tinkling brass.

"She won't start."

"Of course she will. Here, you fellows, give us a push!"

The other crews rallied round to push the heavy vehicle on to the slope in front of the fire station.

" 'Ere, wait for me," gasped Shorty. "I'm supposed to be riding on this 'ere bus."

"Have you got everything now?" a fireman called out, as Shorty's flying leap landed him on the running board.

"Hope so," returned Archie. "We'll have to risk it, anyway; we're about four minutes late getting away. Oh, darn my socks; there'll be a row about this! Okay, boys, give her a shove!"

" 'Ere, 'arf a mo," put in Shorty.

"We can't wait any 'arf mo's," replied Archie.

"But we ain't got no boots."

"What?"

"You told me to take them all orf and we – "

"All right. Here, stop!" he yelled, as the volunteers began the launching ceremony. "Nip off quick, Shorty; you know where you put them."

Panting hard, Fireman Short reached the wellington boots stacked by the *Self-Propelled*. The neat line had been upset by someone in his efforts to hasten the loading, and the boots were all jumbled up.

"Never mind sorting them out," called Cuppling. "Take the first three pairs and sling them up. Oh, get a move on for Pete's sake!" he cried in agony, "it's five minutes since the bells went down."

Shorty seized an armful of boots and climbed aboard. On the slope outside the engine started, somewhat uncertainly, and with the bell ringing furiously, they backfired their way down the High Street at a jerky 15 m.p.h. with the accelerator pressed hard down.

It had taken them six minutes to get out. What would the Column Officer say? Archie blushed beneath his perspiration at the thought of it. And then the more serious side occurred to him. *"Persons believed trapped on top floor."* Heavens! And with the engine misbehaving itself like this they could only make a shaky fifteen miles an hour and there were five miles to be covered!

For three years Leading Fireman Cuppling had looked forward to a job of this kind. He had visualised a perfect turn-out in less than thirty seconds; a 75 m.p.h. dash through the streets; the rescue effected in less time than it takes to tell, with the turntable responding perfectly to his expert touch. And now what a ghastly mess-up it all was! He would probably lose his stripe over it at least, and what if... Cold beads of sweat broke out on his forehead at the thought of the trapped persons anxiously awaiting his arrival.

"Oh, heavens!" he groaned as they rattled past the church and he noted that the clock pointed to one minute past three. "Can't you step on it a bit more, Lofty?"

But Lofty was doing his best, and Archie could only fume and rage, and curse his own misplaced zeal. It was a good thing for his blood pressure that he didn't know that the fire call was a false alarm.

6

The Indian Rope Trick

The Headmaster surveyed the rows of boys lined up before him on the quad.

"Mr Carter," he said, "haven't you finished taking that roll call yet?"

"They're all present, sir, except Dormitory Four," replied Mr Carter. "I can't think what's happened to them."

The Headmaster glanced at his watch.

"Tut-tut! Three o'clock. It must be ten minutes since the gong sounded. What on earth can they be doing?"

Accompanied by Mr Carter and Mr Wilkins, he had watched the other dormitories descending on their escapes in an orderly manner. Everything had gone according to plan, except for the unexplained absence of Dormitory Four.

"You'd better go and see what the matter is, Carter," he said.

Quickly Mr Carter ran up the stairs and found Jennings standing alone at the top.

"Oh, sir, you can't come up these stairs, sir," Jennings began, " 'cos they've fallen in and there's a big hole where you're standing and – "

Mr Carter cut him short.

"What have you been doing all this time?" he demanded.

"You ought all to be outside."

"Well, sir, I went to your room like the Instructions said and as you weren't there I did what you would have done if you had been there; only you weren't, 'cos the Head said you wouldn't be, sir."

"And what would I have done had I been there?"

" 'Phoned for the fire brigade, sir."

It took a few seconds for the full meaning of this to register on Mr Carter's brain.

"In the case of an actual outbreak, of course I should," he began, and then broke off as a horrible thought flashed into his mind. "What!" he gasped. "Jennings, you don't mean you – what exactly have you done, Jennings?"

"Only what the Head said, sir, about using our imagination and all that."

"Oh, imagination!" repeated Mr Carter in relieved tones. "Phew! Thank goodness for that! You gave me quite a turn, Jennings." He felt better now that the horrible thought had turned out to be Jennings' make-believe.

"For the moment I really thought you had 'phoned for the fire brigade. I was just thinking if you really had – ha-ha-ha!" Mr Carter laughed at the fantastic absurdity of such a situation.

"I really have 'phoned them, sir. They ought to be here any minute now."

"Ha-ha-h – ! Whirp!" The laugh was strangled in Mr Carter's throat. A prickly feeling of dismay attacked him in every pore of his skin as the terrible truth spread through his mind.

"Jennings," he said, "you – you silly little boy! Tell me exactly what's happened – quickly."

Jennings told him. With infinite pride he described how he had deduced the Headmaster's intentions; the fallen staircase, the missing master, the smoke-filled building; all had added up neatly and pointed to the turntable ladder as being the only satisfactory solution.

"Oh, my goodness!" said Mr Carter. "Well that has put the cat among the pigeons."

"Haven't I done right, sir?"

"Right? We shall all be prosecuted. False alarm with malicious intent!"

Jennings stopped feeling pleased as Mr Carter delivered himself of a few well-chosen words on the subject of summoning fire brigades when there was nothing for them to do. The fact that Jennings had acted in good faith would not carry much weight when the facts came to light. Jennings felt worse when Mr Carter explained what the Headmaster had really meant. Of course, how silly of him, he had never thought of using the Escape!

Mr Carter groaned in spirit. There was nothing he could do now. It was ten minutes since the silly little boy had sent his message for help and any minute now the clanging of bells would announce the arrival of a crew bursting with eagerness to combat the non-existent flames. Mr Carter could imagine their comments when they were informed that the solid oak staircase on which they were standing didn't exist any more! The Headmaster, too, would take the most serious view of the way in which his orders had been interpreted. The only ray of hope lay in the fact that it was seven minutes past three and there was no sign of the brigade's arrival. Was it possible that they had decided to take no action on the instructions of so youthful a voice on the telephone? It was doubtful, but like a drowning man Mr Carter clutched at this straw of hope – a straw so slender that it would not have broken the back of the weariest of camels.

Jennings by now realised the enormity of his offence.

"Oh, gosh!" he said miserably. "And I was only trying to

use my initiative. How was I to know the Head didn't mean what he said? Will there be an awful row, sir?"

"If they come there'll be a row," said Mr Carter. "A most unholy one."

This was too awful to think about so, like Mr Carter, he seized upon his ray of hope.

"Perhaps they won't come, sir," he said, " 'cos Darbishire says they have baked beans on toast at fire stations, and it has to be a super-important fire before they'll let it get cold – the baked beans I mean, not the fire; and Darbishire ought to know sir, 'cos his father's had a lot of experience with fires, when he's been making toast and that sort of thing, sir."

"If they're not here in a minute or two," said Mr Carter, "there's a chance they won't come." But there was no conviction in his tone.

The Headmaster was a patient man, but he could not wait all day. It was some minutes now since Mr Carter had gone to investigate the mystery of the missing dormitory, and still nothing had happened. At the expense of a slightly ruffled dignity, the Headmaster ran up the stairs and almost collided with Mr Carter on the first landing.

"Oh, there you are, sir," said Mr Carter. "I'm afraid there's been a rather unfortunate misunderstanding, and briefly what's happened is – "

"We haven't time for explanations now, Carter," broke in the Headmaster. "I'm determined to put that dormitory through its escape drill, and it'll be dark before we've finished, at this rate. Go down and take charge on the quad and send Wilkins to me, will you?"

"Yes, but the circumstances are rather exceptional," Mr Carter began again, but found he was addressing the empty air, for the Headmaster had pursued his upward flight towards the top storey, and his expression implied that he was in no mood to stand any nonsense.

Mr Carter shrugged his shoulders. At any moment the blow might fall, but there was nothing anyone could do about it – not even the Headmaster; whereas if the summoned assistance failed to arrive, there was no point in making a song and dance about the telephone message. Not, at any rate, while the Head was in such a testy mood. Later on, all could be explained, if not forgiven and forgotten.

Martin Winthrop Barlow Pemberton-Oakes, MA, Headmaster, flung wide the door of Dormitory No. 4 and stood rooted to the threshold by the sight that met his eyes. Instead of preparing for an orderly evacuation, Temple, Venables, Atkinson and Darbishire, wearing pyjamas over their suits, were crawling round the floor on their stomachs. Their faces were swathed in dripping towels, which left a damp snail's trail behind them as they crawled. Jennings was staring anxiously out of the window with the expression of a prophet foretelling the future, and not liking the look of it.

The Headmaster's face fell like a barometer. Dark rain clouds appeared on the horizon of his countenance, accompanied by a drop in the temperature. A deep depression was approaching; thunderstorms seemed imminent, and the future outlook was anything but settled.

"What on earth are you boys crawling about like that for?"

Like veiled women of the East, the four crawlers arose. Darbishire removed his yashmak.

"Please, sir," he said, "the smoke's not so thick if you keep your nose on the floor, and you can breathe."

"Breathe? Smoke? What are you talking about, and why are you wearing your pyjamas?"

"You said it was the middle of the night, sir," replied Venables.

"It was my fault, sir," said Jennings. "You said pretend it was a real fire and I thought you meant; do everything properly, sir, like sending a message to – well, you see, sir, I'm most terribly sorry, but what actually happened was – "

How on earth could he soften the blow? The expression on the Headmaster's face made it almost impossible for him to proceed at all.

"Well, sir, it's like this, if you see what I mean," he stumbled on, "or rather the point is – "

"The point is, Jennings, that you've behaved in a muddle-headed and irresponsible manner," the Headmaster broke in, giving Jennings no opportunity to confess to the crime which he had unwittingly committed. "When I sent you up here, Jennings, what do you suppose I meant you to use?"

"Our initiatives, sir," replied Jennings.

"Yes, yes, of course; but what else?"

"The 'Pennetra' Fire Escape, sir; Mr Carter just told me."

"Exactly," said the Headmaster. "The whole lot of you are completely unreliable, and I think an extra hour's preparation this evening may help you to think a little more clearly in future."

The burning topic of the fire brigade was still uppermost in Jennings' mind and he made another attempt to explain matters.

"I'm terribly sorry, sir," he said, "and if they do turn up, sir, it won't really be mal-malpractice with intent like Mr Carter said, 'cos I really thought you meant me to; and as they haven't come already, perhaps they won't now, will they, sir?"

As a lucid explanation, there was something lacking in this statement, and having lost so much time already, the Headmaster was in no mood to listen to what he imagined was a rambling apology. Jennings was silenced.

The door burst open with hurricane force and Mr Wilkins approached noisily.

"Mr Carter said you wanted me, sir?"

"Ah, yes, Mr Wilkins. These boys have no idea how to behave at fire drill. Will you kindly explain the working of the Escape to them." And the Headmaster swept out to inspect the other dormitories and to satisfy himself that the great evacuation had left no untidiness in its wake.

For two and a half miles the turntable ladder crawled fitfully along at an uneasy 15 m.p.h., while Archie Cuppling relieved his feelings by ringing the bell continuously and with a savage ferocity. But once out of the town, Lofty put in a complaint.

"You don't have to go on clanging like that on an empty road," he said. "Won't make the old bus go any faster."

"I wish something would," groaned Cupping. "It's quarter of an hour now since we got the 'phone call; ought to have been there ages ago, and got the ladder up by this time. Darn my socks, there won't half be a row about it!" he moaned for the twentieth time.

They were going uphill now, and the speedometer needle dropped back to eight miles per hour.

"She won't take it," said Lofty. "She's conking."

"She's got to take it," Cuppling growled between clenched teeth. He rocked backwards and forwards in his seat in the hope, presumably, that the momentum of his body would give the wheels that extra bit of impetus needed to reach the top of the slope; but it takes an infinite amount of wishful thinking to urge several tons of machinery up a hill when everyone of its fifty-seven horse-power is protesting. The speed dropped to a crawl; the engine gasped, coughed apologetically, and was silent.

Lofty jumped down, hurled open the bonnet and got to work on the carburettor while Archie wrung his hands in despair.

"It'll take me a few minutes," said Lofty, busily wielding a spanner.

"Cor! And another two and a half miles to go yet," groaned his Leading Fireman. "Hurry up for heaven's sake!"

Shorty piped up from behind.

"Let this be a lesson to you," he said. "It don't do to be too efficient. You stick to brass cleaning another time."

"That's enough from you, Fireman Short." Archie had no wish to listen to a lecture on his misdirected enthusiasm. "There's no point in us sitting here like a couple of spare puddings. Come on, we'll be getting our boots on; that'll save a bit of time when we get there."

Fireman Short rummaged amongst the heap of wellingtons and made a suitable selection for his left foot. Then he rummaged again and an air of bewilderment spread across his features.

"That's funny," he said. "I can't find any right boots nowhere; this here boot's a left-footed 'un; so's this 'un; so's this. Well, blow me, if I haven't brought six left boots and no right 'uns!"

Leading Fireman Cuppling groaned inwardly. What had he done to deserve this? What would become of his reputation? He who prided himself on the slickness of his turn-outs and the unruffled efficiency of his firemanship!

"It was you rushing me like that at the last minute," Shorty was saying. "There was about twenty boots, see, all mixed up and you said grab the first six and – "

"All right! All right! You don't have to make a speech about it," the Leading Fireman snapped irritably. "We'll just have to put up with it and wear two left boots. Oh, heavens, it's twelve minutes past three already! We shan't be there before half-past at this rate. Get a move on, Lofty, for Pete's sake; you don't have to take the whole engine to bits, do you?"

"All very well for you to start moaning now, Leading

Fireman Archibald Cuppling," said Lofty bitterly. "If you'd let me get on with cleaning the engine instead of mucking about with wet hose, we shouldn't be stuck where we are now." And Lofty attacked the carburettor ferociously with a screwdriver.

Heaving and straining, Shorty forced an unwilling left boot on to his right foot. It was a size too small and it pinched painfully.

"Cor!" he grumbled. "It don't 'arf give me chilblains the works! I don't want to be what you'd call critical, Leading Fireman," he went on, "but shan't we look a bit daft turning up at a fire all wearing left-'anded gum boots?"

"It'll be something if we get there at all," replied Archie miserably. "When I think of that burning building and those people shouting for help" – Archie's voice throbbed with bitter emotion – "and us still stuck here when we ought to have had the ladder up and the hose run out hours ago…"

"Well, blow me!" interjaculated Shorty. "I just thought of something."

"What is it?"

"We ain't brought no 'ose."

"What???"

"S'right; we got all the dirty 'ose out in the yard, see, and what with all that carry on of loading the bus up, I clean forgot to get some more out of the store."

The Leading Fireman shuddered like a shock absorber under the impact of this new blow, and the faint hope that perhaps someone else had remembered the clean hose was shattered when, with trembling fingers, he flung open the hose lockers. They were as empty as the vessels which make the most sound.

What, Archie asked himself, was the use of having a dozen men to pile on equipment if everyone left the most important item to his neighbour? The delightful proverb of many hands making light work had given place to its terrible sequel of the broth-spoiling cooks. Archie Cuppling was not given to melodrama; he did not tear his hair or beat his breast; neither did he rend his garments. It is doubtful whether he even gave his teeth more than a half-hearted gnash, but he felt justified in asking Fate a question as he stood dejected and left-booted on the roadside.

"Why should this have to happen to me?" he wanted to know.

When Dormitory Four had shed their slumberwear, Mr Wilkins began to expound.

"Now the way this – ah – the way this thing works is extremely simple," he began. "This round metal thing is a container. It contains a coil of cable. And protruding through this aperture here – "

"What, sir?" asked Temple.

"Sticking out of this hole," amended the lecturer, "is a strap, or sling, which goes underneath your armpits. And this – er – gadget here is an adjustable – er – adjuster which you move up and down if you want to adjust it. In other words..." He sought in vain for the correct technical term. "In other words, it's adjustable."

"What's it just able to do, sir?" inquired Venables innocently.

"I didn't say it was just able to do anything."

"Well, what's the good of it, then, sir, if it doesn't do anything?"

"It does do something," said Mr Wilkins irritably. "You sling it along the slide, or rather you slide it along the sling to tighten the strap across your chest so that you don't – er – slide out of the sling."

Mr Wilkins felt he wasn't explaining it very well. However, he pressed on to stage two.

"Now this second sling and coil of cable," he said, "must be slung out of the window before you start, so while you're going down, this other one is coming up ready for the next person, and while he's coming down your sling's going up again." He paused again. It was more than obvious from the blank expressions on all faces that his audience was not with him.

"Is that quite clear?" he asked, knowing it wasn't, but hoping they wouldn't say so.

Venables, Atkinson and Temple knew perfectly well what Mr Wilkins meant as they had been through it all before, but they held their peace.

"But where are you, sir?" asked Darbishire.

"Me? I'm here," replied Mr Wilkins. "I'm going to watch you do it."

"No, not you, sir; me, sir, or whoever it is who gets slung out on the first sling. I mean, when the sling comes up again, doesn't he come up with it?"

"Of course not," said Mr Wilkins. He tried hard to remember the official instructions in the handbook.

"When the – er – the escapee has completed his descent," he quoted, "he disengages the clasp governing the fastenings of the harness and remains on terra firma."

"You mean he slides out of the sling," said Darbishire, summing it up neatly.

Mr Wilkins decided to cancel the remainder of his lecture in favour of a demonstration, so the harness was put round Darbishire's chest and made fast with the adjuster. Mr Wilkins opened the window and threw out the second cable while Darbishire climbed uncertainly on to the window-sill. It looked an uncomfortably long way down to the ground, but if everyone else could do it, he was sure he could. There was just one point, however, on which he wanted reassurance.

"Sir," he said, "what happens if the rope breaks?"

"That's all right, Darbishire," said Temple unfeelingly; "we can easily get another rope."

"It can't break," said Mr Wilkins; "it's a metal cable."

The rest of the dormitory crowded round to speed his departure with words of comfort.

"I say, Darbishire," said Venables cheerfully, "just supposing we don't see you again, could I have your four-bladed penknife?" And he smiled like an undertaker who scents a likely client.

"Don't be such a ruin," said Darbishire. "I shall be all right. My father says – "

"Off you go, then, Darbishire," said Mr Wilkins. "You go down quite slowly. Get into a kneeling position with your feet behind you and push yourself gently away from the wall as you go down."

"Why, sir?" asked Darbishire, suspecting some new trap for the unwary.

"You've got to keep clear of the ivy that's growing up the wall; you don't want to get caught up on that, do you?"

"Hadn't I better just make a famous last speech, sir, like John of Gaunt and Sidney Carton, and all that lot?" said Darbishire, savouring the dramatic possibilities of the situation.

"Are you going to get out of that window or aren't you?" demanded Mr Wilkins impatiently.

"Oh, yes, sir. I was only going to – well, goodbye chaps," said Darbishire hurriedly, catching sight of Mr Wilkins' expression. "This is a far, far better thing I do than I have ever done." Kneeling on thin air he launched out into space and disappeared slowly from sight as the Escape whirred into action.

"It is a far, far better place I go to than I have ever known." His famous last speech became fainter and finally faded out altogether.

Unfortunately, Darbishire forgot to push himself gently from the wall and keep his legs in a kneeling position, with the result that some five seconds later his feet touched down unexpectedly on the window-sill of the room immediately below his dormitory. He was wondering whether the sill would make a suitable runway for a fresh take-off, when a thought flashed into his mind and, releasing the clasp that secured him to the sling, he climbed in through the open window of Dormitory Two.

"It was lucky I thought of it in time," he told himself. If this drill was to be a dress rehearsal for the real thing, no detail should be left incomplete, and, in the excitement of the moment, he had left his four-bladed penknife, with corkscrew, behind in his dormitory. He would never have left that to be lost in the flames, so it was jolly lucky he had remembered it while there was still time to go back. Leaving the cable hanging outside the window, he climbed into the empty dormitory and started to make his way back to his own room.

Mr Wilkins was somewhat surprised when the whirr of the Escape stopped abruptly some five seconds after Darbishire's departure. He had just been saying how easy it all was, and was prophesying a happy landing for Darbishire some quarter of a minute after being airborne. Something had gone wrong with the estimated time of arrival and, distinctly puzzled, Mr Wilkins put his head out of the window for a quick reconnaissance. A strangled cry of amazement rattled its way through his vocal cords.

"Glip!" he gulped. There, swinging gently in the breeze some fifteen feet below, was the sling which should have contained a boy, but the boy had vanished.

Mr Wilkins looked down, but Darbishire was not on the ground below; Mr Wilkins looked sideways and even upwards, though this was hardly necessary.

"I – I – I – What – what – what – I don't understand… It's not possible… It just can't be."

The rest of the boys gathered round the window with suitable queries on their faces, but none could explain the mystery.

"Perhaps it's a new version of the Indian rope trick," vouchsafed Jennings; "only instead of going up a rope, Darbishire's invented a way of doing it backwards."

The door opened and the Headmaster appeared. He had finished inspecting the other dormitories, and had missed Darbishire's dramatic entry through the window below, by a few seconds.

"What's the matter, Mr Wilkins?" he asked. "Is anything wrong?"

"I'm glad you've come, sir," replied Mr Wilkins. "I'm seeing things, or rather I'm not seeing things; not the things I ought to be seeing, if you see what I mean."

The Headmaster didn't, and Mr Wilkins endeavoured to explain, but so much was wholly inexplicable, and his manner was so agitated, that the Headmaster refused to believe him.

"Disappeared, Mr Wilkins?" he said. "Nonsense; he can't have." And striding to the window he, too, looked down upon an empty sling.

"Good heavens!" he said. "Are you quite sure you put him in the sling to start with?"

Mr Wilkins called upon the remainder of the dormitory as witnesses.

"But it's unheard of," said the Headmaster. "The cable's all right; the sling's all right; it's uncanny; it's…"

The dormitory door opened and Darbishire walked in.

It is difficult to describe the emotions aroused by his dramatic entrance. Shakespeare might have done it with a flourish of trumpets, and hautboys without, but the printed word can hardly do justice to the stupefied reaction of Messrs Pemberton-Oakes, Wilkins and party.

The Headmaster was the first to recover the power of speech.

"Where have you been, Darbishire?" he demanded. Darbishire couldn't think why everyone was staring at him in so marked a fashion.

"Nowhere, sir," he said.

His audience were almost ready to believe that nowhere was the right answer, and that Darbishire had been spirited away by fairy hands to some nonexistent locality, but the Headmaster prosaically demanded details.

"Nowhere special, I mean, sir," said Darbishire. "You see, I was coming down on the Escape and approaching Dorm Two window, sir, and suddenly, before I knew where I was, I'd…" He stopped. What a good job he had remembered the penknife in time; the Headmaster would be ever so pleased with this conscientious regard for detail.

"Go on," prompted the Headmaster. "Before you knew where you were – ?"

"Oh, I did know where I was, really, sir, like my father did when he was making toast in the kitchen that time."

The Headmaster failed to understand why Darbishire's father making toast in the kitchen should have any bearing on his son's mysterious disappearance. Darbishire explained, but he was doomed to disappointment if he thought that salvage operations for four-bladed penknives would be accepted as a good reason for returning to a burning building.

"You came back?" said the Headmaster incredulously.

"Yes, sir."

The Headmaster turned on his irony.

"What an intellect!" he murmured. "What a masterly

grasp of the correct procedure to be followed when evacuating a burning building. You came back! I congratulate you!"

Darbishire smiled modestly and was about to express his thanks in a few well-chosen words, but a glance at the Headmaster's expression showed him that the time was not ripe. He made a hurried alteration in the programme and cancelled the vote of thanks.

"Would it be placing too great a strain on your intelligence, Darbishire," the Headmaster continued, "to ask you to consider why returning to this dormitory after you had already left it, was a stupid mistake?"

Darbishire thought. Surely you weren't expected to leave four-bladed penknives behind to be consumed by the nearest flame? It must be something else he had done.

"Oh, yes, I know, sir," he said brightly. "I came back up the stairs that weren't there. Yes, that was rather silly of me. Oh, but, sir, you must have come up those stairs, too, sir, so either I did right or we both made stu – er – we both committed errors of judgment, sir."

"You can be exasperatingly stupid at times, Darbishire. The cardinal error you committed was to come back to a supposedly burning building. 'Life before property' is the motto of all good firemen."

"Oh, gosh!" said Jennings suddenly. "I'd forgotten the firemen." By twisting his head until it was nearly upside down, he could see the time by Mr Wilkins' wristwatch. It was twenty-one minutes past three.

"Well, that settles it," he said to himself. "They won't be coming now."

Jennings spoke too soon. On a lonely stretch of road some two and a half miles away, Fireman Long was putting the finishing touches to his handiwork. The carburettor had not been in a co-operative mood, and it had taken him longer than he had anticipated. This delay had done nothing to improve Leading Fireman Cuppling's frame of mind. He stared up and down the road in the hope of seeing a car whose aid he could summon. By this means he, at least, could get to the scene of the fire and see what was happening, and leave the turntable ladder to follow when it was ready. Unfortunately, it was a lonely stretch of road and no traffic had passed during the anxious minutes of the breakdown. Archie knew, too, that there was no telephone for two miles in either direction, so he was unable to send a message for assistance to the fire station. They were stranded; the situation was hopeless. All they could do was to wait until Lofty's skill had changed the engine from an inert mass of metal to a high-powered machine.

Archie had decided not to go back for the hose; after all, the rescue was the most important job to be tackled, and the ladder at any rate, was in working order.

It was twenty-two minutes past three when Lofty leaped back into the driver's seat and pressed the starter.

"She's okay now," he said. The engine leaped to life and, in his skilful hands, the speedometer needle crept up, fifty, sixty, seventy miles per hour. Archie rang the bell as though his life depended on it; as it happened other lives did, for farm hands and stray cows had only just time to hurl themselves to safety in the hedge as the turntable ladder flashed past. But whatever their speed now, nothing could make up for earlier delays. It would be three twenty-five before they got to Linbury; thirty-four minutes to answer a five-mile call. Horrors!

Fireman Long's eye was glued to the road and his hands were glued to the steering wheel, but his tongue was by no means glued to his mouth.

"You haven't half done it this time, Leading Fireman Cuppling, Esq," he yelled, and his voice was scarcely audible above the clanging of the bell. "You haven't half boxed it all up nicely. Getting to a fire half an hour late, at fifteen blinking miles an hour, with no hose and all wearing left-footed boots. I wouldn't be in your shoes when we get back."

"I wouldn't mind whose shoes I was in," said Shorty, clinging to the ladder for dear life, "so long as they wasn't these 'ere left 'anded gum boots. Cor! They aren't 'arf letting me chilblains know about it."

On they thundered, ready and eager to get to grips with the fire which, after all this time, must be a raging inferno, and worthy of the attention of the most intrepid of fire fighters. How one got to grips with such a situation when one had no hose was, of course, a debatable point, but Archie's determination was such that he felt ready to beat out the flames with his bare hands, if such a course could restore his lost prestige. Seventy-three, seventy-four, seventy-five miles per hour read the speedometer, as they streaked through the countryside on their life-saving pilgrimage.

7

Suspense and Suspension

"Mr Wilkins," said the Headmaster when he had finished rebuking Darbishire, "these boys seem to have no idea of what is expected of them in an emergency. Will you kindly demonstrate the correct method of descending by the Escape."

"Certainly, sir," said Mr Wilkins. Rapidly he hauled in the cable, fastened himself into the sling, and leapt on to the window-sill.

"Now watch me carefully, you boys," boomed the demonstrator, "and you'll see how easy it is." They crowded round the window and Mr Wilkins disappeared from view with his commentary still running.

"Now I want you to observe how I push myself..." The running commentary suddenly ceased. So did the whirr of the Escape as, for the second time, an unrehearsed incident enlivened the proceedings.

"Gosh, it's stopped again!" said Temple.

"What's happened?" asked Darbishire, from the rear of the group.

"Stand back, you boys," said the Headmaster, thrusting them aside and leaning out of the window.

An unfortunate occurrence had marred what would otherwise have been a perfect demonstration. Mr Wilkins, directing the stream of his commentary to the window above his head, had omitted to push himself gently away from the wall, and the strap across his chest had caught on a thick branch of ivy. To his chagrin, he found himself suspended in midair. Mr Wilkins struggled to free himself, but his efforts bore no fruit. The weight of his body kept the cable taut and, without a foothold, he was unable to slacken the tension and unhook himself; the branch of ivy was strong and showed no tendency to break. It was an uncomfortable, though not a dangerous, situation, and certainly not one to assist the dignity of the expert demonstrator.

"What's happened, Mr Wilkins?" inquired the Headmaster, somewhat unnecessarily.

Snatches of semi-audible comment and a muffled "Cor-wumph" drifted up to the group in the dormitory above.

"It's no good," called Mr Wilkins, after further battle with the ivy. "The sling's caught tight, and I can't get any leverage on the branch to break it."

Headmasters are admirable in crises. Action, prompt and immediate, was the watchword of M W B Pemberton-Oakes, Esq. He seized on the nearest boy, who happened to be Jennings, and gave his orders in a crisp and concise manner.

"Quick," he said. "Run and find Robinson and tell him to bring a ladder. Explain that Mr Wilkins is suspended, like the sword of Damocles, on an obstinate tendril of ivy."

"Suspended on a what, like whose sword, sir?" inquired Jennings.

"Never mind what," said the Headmaster. "Just tell him to bring his longest ladder, and be quick about it. Explain that Mr Wilkins is caught up sixty feet above ground level."

Jennings rushed off in quest of old Pyjams, while the Headmaster satisfied himself that Mr Wilkins was in no immediate danger.

"You're sure you can't release yourself?" he called.

A disgruntled "Cor-wumph" from below implied that, if Mr Wilkins had been able to release himself, he would have done so, and that he was not dangling sixty feet above the ground purely for his own selfish pleasure.

"Rotten luck, isn't it, sir?" said Atkinson.

"Most unfortunate," agreed the Headmaster. "I shall certainly get Robinson to cut all this ivy down, first thing tomorrow."

"What's that you said?" called Mr Wilkins from below.

The Headmaster raised his voice.

"I was saying I shall have the ivy cut down tomorrow."

"Tomorrow?" echoed Mr Wilkins. "But, bless me, I can't stay here all night!"

The Headmaster leaned further out of the window and issued a communiqué to the effect that Operation Rescue would receive priority treatment, and steps were even now being taken to ensure a satisfactory solution to the problem. After that, they tried to pull Mr Wilkins up; they heaved and gasped and strained, but the odds were against them, for not only did Mr Wilkins weigh thirteen stone, but also the branch of ivy was holding the sling in such a way that pulling on the cable merely tightened its grip.

Soon Jennings returned with the disquieting news that old Pyjams – he begged sir's pardon, he meant Robinson – could not help. The longest ladder on the premises was only thirty feet and would not reach anywhere near the top floor. Furthermore, Robinson begged to state that he had never heard of the sword of whoever it was, and doubted whether it would be much use, anyway.

"Most annoying," exclaimed the Headmaster. "We ought to have a sixty-foot ladder on the premises. I shall certainly order one the next time I go to London."

From below, Mr Wilkins demanded to be kept abreast of

the latest developments.

"What did you say, then?" he called.

"I said I'm going to order a ladder the next time I go to London."

"Yes, but good heavens – I mean, dash it, sir – I can't go on hanging here all that time!"

"This is an intolerable situation," said the Headmaster. He could not leave Mr Wilkins to cool his heels indefinitely. Ah, he had it!

"I shall telephone the fire station immediately," he said, "and request them to send a long ladder, without delay."

It is said that opportunity knocks once at the door of every man. Jennings heard the knock and answered it.

"Please, sir," he said; "I've done that already."

"You've telephoned for the fire brigade?" said the Headmaster, in surprise.

"Yes, sir; you see, I was trying to use my initiative and I thought – ".

"Thank you, Jennings. I congratulate you. Your action was perhaps a little unorthodox, but with Mr Wilkins in his precarious position I'm inclined to agree that there was no time to be lost."

The Headmaster looked at Jennings with a new interest. He had misjudged him. How many other boys, he wondered, on hearing that Robinson's ladder was too short, would have had the initiative to rush forthwith to the telephone and call for assistance.

Jennings felt he ought to explain that the telephone call was due to his stupidity; that he had made it half an hour before, and that the fire brigade weren't coming, anyway. But, basking in the glory of the Headmaster's congratulations, he decided that this was not the moment to start shattering anyone's illusions.

"Let me see," said the Headmaster, consulting his watch.

"H'm. Let us say that it is three, or perhaps four, minutes since you telephoned; they have roughly five miles to come, so that even if they started at once, we can hardly expect them to be here for another..." He broke off abruptly as the distant clanging of a fire bell caught his ear. It was not often that Martin Winthrop Barlow Pemberton-Oakes, Headmaster, betrayed his feelings, but now his eyes opened wide in bewilderment. There could be no doubt of it, the clanging was louder now. In two strides the Headmaster reached the window and was just in time to see a fire engine swing round the corner and come tearing up the drive.

"Well, I – bless my – words fail me," he said, and hurried out to direct operations from below.

What an amazingly efficient brigade, he thought, as he took the non-existent stairs two at a time. They must have left the fire station a split second after receiving the call, and streaked along the roads like a flash of lightning.

The turntable ladder skidded round the bend of the drive on two wheels and pulled up outside the main entrance with a screeching of brakes.

"Can't see any fire," said Lofty. "I reckon it's got tired of waiting for us and burnt itself out. What do you think, Shorty?"

"I don't think," replied Fireman Short. "I'm that uncomfortable with me right foot stuck in this left-'anded boot, it's made me so numb I can't think."

The Headmaster was approaching at a brisk pace. Archie leapt smartly to meet him.

"Turntable ladder; Leading Fireman Cuppling in charge," he said.

He was surprised at the warm welcome expressed in the Headmaster's answering smile. He had been expecting a fusillade of complaints; a volley of criticism; a broadside of angry protestation at the unforgivable delay: in short, anything but a smile.

"Excellent, excellent," beamed the Headmaster. "You have been quick! We sent for you because one of our assistant masters is in a state of suspension just round here." And he led him round the corner and pointed upwards to where Mr Wilkins appeared to be flowering amongst the ivy.

"Is that all, sir?" inquired the Leading Fireman.

"It's enough, isn't it?" replied the Headmaster.

"I mean, no fire or anything like that?" persisted Archie.

"No, no fire; nothing like that."

It seemed too good to be true; surely there was a catch in it somewhere. But there was no catch, and in a matter of seconds the turntable was in position.

"Get to work!" shouted Archie. In his skilful hands the ladder responded like some prehistoric monster roused from sleep. Strong legs unwound themselves and planted feet of steel firmly on the ground to take the strain of the monster's weight; the ladder rose from the gantry as though the beast were lifting its head and stretching its serpentine neck.

Lofty was on the tiny platform at the head of the ladder, and he shot rapidly skywards as Archie accelerated, and the creature's growl became a whine. By this time the entire school had congregated on the quad. With bated breath and eyes agog, they watched the monstrous neck spanning the space between the ground and Mr Wilkins' rapidly cooling heels, as Archie's deft fingers on the controls worked miracles of extension and elevation. Gently, the neck craned forward and came to rest alongside Mr Wilkins.

With his feet solidly on the ladder, it was the work of a moment for Mr Wilkins, assisted by Lofty, to free himself from the sling, and a minute later both men were safely on the ground.

A buzz of excited chatter broke the tension as soon as the rescue was completed. Breath was 'unbated' and eyes were 'ungogged' as everywhere the conversation turned upon the topic of the moment.

"Super-duper, smashing priority prang, wasn't it?" said Brown major.

"Yes, hefty spivish," agreed Thompson minor.

"Hairy famous, too," added Rumbelow. "And wizard decent of old Wilkie to get stuck specially so's we could see him rescued."

"I wish I'd thought of it when I was coming down," put in Darbishire. "It'd be prangish rare to come down on the turntable. Why do masters have all the luck?"

Mr Wilkins felt that he had received enough notoriety for one afternoon and would have preferred to have made an unobtrusive exit, but he was unable to evade the admiring throng that crowded round him.

"You are lucky, sir! Was it nice up there, sir?"

"Sir, did you mean to get stuck so's we could see how the fire brigade worked, sir?"

"Sir, are you going to do it again, because you didn't really finish coming down on the sling, sir."

"Perhaps you didn't bend your knees and push the wall hard enough, sir."

"Sir, if you push the wall too hard you might get into a tail spin, mightn't you, sir?"

"All right, all right. Be quiet," said Mr Wilkins, and turning to Leading Fireman Cuppling, rendered suitable thanks for his deliverance.

"That's all right, sir," said Archie. "I'm sorry you had to stay up there so long."

Mr Wilkins assured him that the inconvenience had been trifling, and that he was none the worse for it.

They must be tough, these schoolmasters, Archie decided. Stranded for over half an hour on the end of the cable was certainly no joke, and this chap seemed as fit and hearty as though he'd been up there only a few minutes.

Now that the rescue was over, Archie had time to think. So far they had had a lucky escape; as there was no fire to extinguish, the question of the forgotten hose did not arise, but the unheard of delay of thirty-five minutes in answering the call could not be so easily forgotten. He decided to find out how serious a view the Headmaster was taking.

"Excuse me, sir," he said hesitantly. "I suppose there's no chance of your overlooking what time we arrived, is there?"

"There certainly isn't," replied the Headmaster genially.

"You mean you're going to report it to the fire station?"

"Most definitely," replied the Headmaster.

Archie's spirits dropped. Of course, no one could be expected to overlook such an interminable delay. There would be an official inquiry. He would have to write endless reports and he would be certain to find himself charged with neglect of duty... He forced his attention back to the Headmaster and listened with growing amazement to his words. What on earth was the chap talking about?

"...and I shall certainly write to your Commanding Officer," he was saying, "and tell him how impressed I was by the speed of your arrival. Why, you must have left the station in a flash and swept through the town like a rocket."

Archie rocked slightly on his heels and gripped the turntable for support.

"Well, darn my socks!" he muttered.

"And your gallant crew as well," proceeded the Headmaster, indicating Firemen Long and Short with a sweep of the hand. "I shall certainly mention the verve and aplomb with which they carried out the rescue."

"What's that he's saying?" whispered Shorty.

"He says we rescued the bloke with verve and aplomb."

"No, we never," said Shorty. "We used the turntable. I

reckon we must have left the verve and what he said, behind with the 'ose."

A look of concern passed over the Headmaster's features as his eye rested on Fireman Short.

"You appear to be limping," he said. "I do trust you haven't injured yourself in effecting the rescue."

"That's all right, guv'nor," replied Shorty. "It's only these 'ere left gum boots."

Leading Fireman Cuppling felt it was time to go before more questions were asked. He did not understand why their unfortunate chapter of accidents should be regarded as a triumphant achievement, but if ever there was a time for letting sleeping dogs lie, this was it. He muttered something about his chief's concern at their being away so long.

The Headmaster laughed heartily at this pleasantry and delivered an apt quotation from the classics to prove that their phenomenal speed must surely be due to their borrowing the winged shoes of Mercury.

"If these 'ere left-'anded gum boots belong to Mercury," grumbled Shorty, "he can keep 'em." And he climbed aboard and massaged his right foot.

Just as they were about to start, Jennings asked the Headmaster whether he might put a question to the Leading Fireman.

"Certainly," smiled the Headmaster. "What is it? Some mechanical intricacy of the turntable which has set your mind wondering?"

"No, sir," replied Jennings. "I want to ask him why all firemen have to have two left feet. Of course, it must be super for playing outside left, but how would you keep in step when you were doing PT?"

"Don't be frivolous, Jennings," replied the Headmaster as Archie blushed a delicate pink and looked uncomfortable. "Now, if you had some sensible question to ask, about the

'Pennetra' Escape, for instance, I'm sure the Leading Fireman knows a lot about Escapes, isn't that so, Leading Fireman?"

"Yes, sir," replied Archie meaningly. "And I think I've just had a very lucky one."

Lofty let in the clutch and the appliance disappeared round the bend of the drive.

The school was despatched from the quad and the boys dispersed to busy themselves with various occupations designed, in the words of the Headmaster, to develop their creative faculties. Some tinkered with bits of wire and cats' whiskers, as home-made wireless sets took shape; others strove with chisels and balsa wood to produce models of Spanish galleons, and others again hacked with blunt knives at odd strips of leather and produced shapeless objects that defied description. The last were usually designed as Christmas presents for fond aunts, who used them to wedge windows in draughty Tudor cottages.

The thrilling rescue of Mr Wilkins was still the main topic of conversation and would be for days, but Darbishire was worried about a matter of pressing importance and went in search of Jennings to ask his advice. He found Jennings kneading an unwilling piece of damp clay. The finished product was going to be either an ashtray for his father or a china nest egg for a poultry-keeping godmother – depending on which article his handiwork most resembled when it was finished.

"What are you looking so worried about, Darbishire?" he asked.

"It's about my Cake List," said Darbishire. "I've been making a Cake List ever since the beginning of term, of all the people I've promised a bit of cake to when my grandmother's parcel came." He produced, for Jennings' inspection, a large and crumpled sheet of paper headed Cake

List in block capitals. There were some forty names, nearly all of which had been crossed out and filled in again two or three times.

"It's like this," he explained. "When a chap's been smashing decent to me, I put his name on my Cake List, and then, if he incurs my serious displeasure after that, I cross him off again."

It had sounded simple enough when Darbishire had worked it out, but in practice snags arose which he had not foreseen. For instance, Temple had been placed on the List for lending Darbishire a piece of blotting paper, but when on the following day he had called Darbishire a "radio-active suet pudding," he was informed that his name had been expunged from the roll. Temple's answer to this was that unless he was re-admitted to the ranks of the chosen, Darbishire would be bashed up forthwith. Might conquered right, and Temple was reinstated, and his policy was immediately adopted by everyone else. Those who were on the List threatened reprisals if they were crossed off, and those who were not included in the first place, hinted darkly at what would happen if their names were not added.

"So you see the mess up it all is," ended Darbishire sadly. "I started off thinking it was a wizard wheeze to reward virtue and keep everyone friendly, but now I've had to put all sorts of bogus oiks on the List, just to protect myself."

Jennings agreed that this was unfortunate, but could not see why Darbishire regarded the matter with such anxiety.

"Well," said Darbishire, "my grandmother's cake came this morning, and I'm going to take it in to tea today, and if you come and have a look at it, you'll jolly well see how urgent it is."

Jennings left his masterpiece of clay, and together they went down to the tuck-box room.

"There," said Darbishire, throwing back the lid of his

tuck-box. "You see what I mean, don't you?"

Jennings saw. Possibly, Darbishire's grandmother had intended the small sponge cake for her grandson alone. Certainly, she had not reckoned on supplying forty clamouring Cake List claimants. The cake measured barely six inches in diameter and was about an inch thick,

"How on earth is that going round forty people?" demanded Darbishire. "Mind you, I'm very grateful, but you would think grandmothers had more sense, wouldn't you!"

"Why not cross some of the names off the List, then," suggested Jennings.

Darbishire sighed. Most of the boys were bigger than he was, and to cross names off at random was asking for trouble. He frowned hard at the List.

"You can cross off Perry and Alsop and Binns minor, and Plackett," said Jennings. "They won't kick up much of a fuss because they're smaller than you are."

"Yes, I know," replied Darbishire; "but I put those four on because they were decent, and not because of what they said they'd do if I didn't."

Darbishire battled hard with his conscience; it seemed unfair to cross chaps off just because they were mild and inoffensive and leave others on for fear of offending them.

"No," he said resolutely, "those four are going to stay and four others can come off." He closed his eyes and made four random strokes across the List with a pencil. It was not a success the first time, for the words he crossed out included Jennings, Cake List, Venables, and the date. But at last he had reduced the roll to a round three dozen.

"Now what?" he demanded.

Jennings had an idea. Both the boys had started to learn geometry, and here was a chance to put their knowledge to the test.

"There are three hundred and sixty degrees in a circle," he

announced. He knew this because he had had to write it out twenty-five times for Mr Wilkins.

"All right, then, if there are thirty-six people on the Cake List, they can have ten degrees each."

"Gosh! Yes, of course," said Darbishire, impressed.

They rushed off to their classroom and returned with protractor, ruler and compass. The discovery had shattered the popular belief that mathematics was of no practical value. With the protractor laid centrally across the cake, they pricked tiny holes with the point of the compass at ten-degree intervals round the circumference.

Ten-degree portions of cake looked somewhat inadequate when the measuring up process was finished, and seemed to bear little resemblance to the theoretical calculations.

"Well, anyway," said Jennings as the tea bell sounded, "there'll be a titchy hunk all round, so no one'll have any reason to grumble."

Darbishire bore his cake proudly to the dining-hall, while Jennings carried the geometrical instruments in case of dispute.

"Of course, it's all very well to work it out on paper," said Darbishire, when the first course was finished, "but somehow I don't think those ten degree hunks are going to work." As he wielded the knife, he was conscious of the eyes of thirty-six shareholders awaiting their dividend.

"You see, we didn't allow for the thickness of the knife, and all these crumbs."

"It just proves what I've always said," remarked Jennings. "Geom. and Maths and stuff, only works out in exercise books. It goes to pieces completely the moment you try to make it do something sensible."

"It couldn't go to pieces any more than this cake is," said Darbishire. "Look, Jen, these hunks are coming out all wrong. It strikes me we've either got to cut the beastly cake

112

into four decent sized pieces or thirty-six large crumbs." He sliced it into four quarters and sighed at the impossible task which lay ahead. It would take a precision instrument of the utmost delicacy to cut each of the resulting slices into nine wafers.

"I tell you what," said Jennings. "I'll take it up to Matron and see if she can cut it up small like you want it."

He seized the plate with the four slices and trotted up to the top table where Matron was standing in earnest conversation with Mr Carter. But before Jennings got there, the door opened and the Headmaster entered and joined the two adults by the top table. Thereupon, all three embarked upon a lengthy discussion on the uninteresting subject of whether Parslow major should be punished for losing his football socks, or whether Mrs Parslow was the real criminal for sending her son to school without having sewn his name on the offending articles.

Jennings hung about diffidently on the edge of the discussion group hoping to catch Matron's eye, but he was unsuccessful. Eventually, the Headmaster turned round and saw Jennings at his elbow, holding a plate containing four slices of sponge cake of medium size.

"Oh," he said. "Is this for me? How very nice!" It was impossible for Jennings to say no, so he smiled a sickly smile as the Headmaster innocently helped himself to the rations of nine hopeful shareholders.

"Very kind of you," smiled the Headmaster. He had not the slightest desire to eat any cake, but he felt that it would be churlish to refuse and might hurt the boy's feelings, so he forced himself to do his duty.

"Excellent cake, don't you think so, Matron?" he inquired.

Matron could not say, not having sampled it, so Jennings took the only course left to him and offered a piece to her and a third one to Mr Carter. He caught Darbishire's eye and felt he wasn't handling the situation very well, but what else could he do? The thirty-six interested parties watched with horror as the cake was demolished, with some effort, by the three grown-ups. None of the three realised the havoc that they were causing; they didn't even know that the plate contained the total sum of grandmother Darbishire's generosity, but supposed them to be slices cut from a larger cake.

Darbishire goggled in wide-eyed amazement. What on earth did Jennings think he was doing? There was still one slice left, but by this time, Darbishire's mistrust was so pronounced that he would not have been surprised had the traitorous Jennings presented the remaining portion to the housekeeper's cat.

The Headmaster swallowed the last of his cake.

"Ah, Jennings, yes," he said, "that reminds me." He called for silence, and those whose appetites had not been destroyed by the horrifying spectacle they had just witnessed, stopped eating and gave ear.

"This afternoon," he began, "our fire practice was enlivened by an unusual incident which was beyond our control. However, the prompt action of Jennings in telephoning for the fire brigade meant that Mr Wilkins suffered only slight inconvenience. Now, there is an excellent example of using one's initiative, and I congratulate you, Jennings, on your resource and intelligence. That doesn't mean," he went on hurriedly, "that boys may normally use the telephone without permission, but this was an exceptional occasion, and Jennings rose to it with exceptional verve and aplomb." He paused, remembering the scene in the dormitory before Mr Wilkins' mishap.

"Earlier on," he proceeded, "I had had occasion to be dissatisfied with the boys of Dormitory Four, and I awarded an extra hour's prep in consequence, but I have now decided to cancel this imposition, as I feel that such outstanding initiative should be rewarded. Don't you agree, Mr Carter?" he asked, turning to his assistant for confirmation.

Mr Carter's conscience told him that he didn't agree at all. On the other hand it seemed a pity to be a wet blanket when everyone was so pleased with the way things had turned out. Carter versus Conscience was a keen contest, and Conscience won on points.

"Well, sir," he began, "there is another aspect of the matter which seems to have escaped your notice – "

"No, no, no, Mr Carter," broke in the Headmaster. "Let us not be niggardly. Honour where honour is due. In fact," he went on in a sudden burst of generosity, "I think it would be fitting to excuse the whole school from evening preparation as a token that I am not slow to recognise meritorious conduct."

Seventy-eight pairs of hands clapped loudly, while Jennings clutched the cake plate and cast his eyes downwards, with becoming modesty.

It was not until the following day that Mr Carter discovered the true facts about the Cake List calamity. Darbishire had managed to salvage the fourth piece of cake for himself, but he had had a difficult time in explaining the facts to those who had hoped for a share. Mr Carter felt a little guilty, so he went into the town and bought Darbishire a cake, and this time the diameter was twelve inches and the depth was five.

Darbishire thanked Mr Carter in a dozen different positions and ambled happily out of Mr Carter's room hugging the gift tightly. But a moment later he was back.

"Please, sir," he said, "have you got such a thing as a large piece of paper I could have."

"I think so. How about this sheet of exam paper?"

"Thank you very much, sir," said Darbishire.

He deposited the cake in his tuck-box and took the sheet of paper to his classroom and sat down at his desk.

"Revised Cake List," he wrote in block capitals. "The following persons on the list here below can get one bit per head but not if they do not be decent:

1. Mr Carter
2. Jennings
3. Venables
4.   "

The tea bell rang just as he finished the List, and Jennings appeared.

"I say, Darbi," he said, "would you like me to help you cut your cake up and hand it round?"

"No jolly fear," said Darbishire.

8

The Literary Masterpiece

Half-term came, and with it a break in the routine of going into class, and changing for football; of being called by one's surname, and saying "Yes, sir." For one weekend this could be forgotten, and yet it was impossible to forget. One weekend wasn't long enough to change anyone from a unit in a boarding school to a member of a family; and new parents who arrived expecting to find their sons the same as they were at home, were puzzled and sometimes disappointed.

When half-term Saturday dawned, the boys rose eager and excited, and put on their best suits. Heads were sleeked with unaccustomed smears of hair cream, and Matron gave ear crevices a critical survey before she passed any boy as fit to go out with his parents. Matron's inspection was thorough; she examined them tooth and nail, and woe betide any miserable specimen who tried to slip past with a missing shirt button, or high-tide marks at wrist or neck.

The Reverend and Mrs Darbishire arrived from the wilds of Hertfordshire, forearmed with questions about academic progress and winter-weight underwear.

Mr and Mrs Jennings motored over from Haywards Heath, eager for every detail of their son's new way of life.

"I'm so excited about seeing him again," Mrs Jennings said

to her husband as the car passed through Dunhambury. "I'm just dying to hear all about it; we'll let him talk while we just sit back and listen; won't it be fun!"

"I expect he'll be full of it," replied her husband. "I'm looking forward to hearing how he's getting on with his work. I'll get him to let me know if he's having difficulty with any of his lessons."

"Do you think I ought to see Matron about his going to bed early if he feels tired?"

"Well, let's see what he has to say first."

But they were doomed to disappointment. Jennings had plenty to say, and didn't propose to waste time talking about such dull subjects as Algebra and cough-mixture; and all their efforts to probe what they considered to be the more important side of school life, were promptly side-tracked. They had to listen, instead, to a long account of why Venables had had to come down to breakfast wearing his pyjama jacket because his shirt fell in the wash-basin.

"Yes, dear, I'm sure that must have been very awkward for him," said Mrs Jennings; "but what we want to know is whether you're settling down all right; how do you like being at a boarding school?"

"Oh, it's all right, thanks."

"And have you made lots of nice friends?"

"Oh, yes; they're all right, thanks."

"How about your appetite? Are you eating well?"

"Oh, yes, all right. I say, Atkinson's got a super blister on his ankle." Jennings felt it was time to turn the conversation to more interesting topics.

"How are you getting on in school; top of the form yet?" inquired his father.

"No, not yet. He's going to have it lanced on Tuesday, and Matron says Atkinson's blister is the – "

"How do you like learning French?"

118

"Oh, all right. Bod's got a super wizzo frog; it's got sort of yellow spot things all down its back."

"And is Mr Carter giving you your pocket money every week?"

"Yes... He keeps it behind the boot-lockers."

"Behind the boot-lockers?" echoed his father. "It doesn't sound a very safe place to me."

"Oh, it can't get away," Jennings explained. "It's in a cardboard box with moss and wet leaves."

"Are you talking about your pocket money?" asked his father.

"No, the frog; it's spivish rare. Bod was told to get rid of it 'cos he took it into the common-room. The Head made an ozard hoo-hah about it." Jennings laughed at the recollection, and his mind rushed off at a tangent.

"It was wizard," he said. "When he laughs he's got a gold tooth."

Mr Jennings was left to speculate whether the gold tooth belonged to the Headmaster, Bod or the frog, and where it went when the owner was not laughing, for Jennings had already launched out on the story of how Brown minor had filled an ink-well with stale cake crumbs. But of himself, of the things they had come to hear, there was scarcely a word. Questions about his welfare were answered briefly with, "All right, thanks," or "Pretty ozard," or "Supersonic."

They all enjoyed the weekend with its lunches in hotels, and teas in cafés, and drives in the car, but, when it was all over, Mr and Mrs Jennings returned home baffled. They had no more knowledge of the things that really mattered than when they had started.

"What are we going to tell Grandma?" said Mrs Jennings on the way home. "She'll be dying to know all the details."

Mr Jennings accelerated to pass a lorry.

"We'll just have to pass on the information as we got it,"

119

he said helplessly, "and see if she can make anything of it."

Grandma greeted them excitedly when they stepped out of the car.

"Well," she beamed, "and how is the dear boy?"

"Oh, all right, thanks," said Mr Jennings.

"Only all right?" queried Grandma, suspecting the worst.

"Not too ozard," put in Mrs Jennings, struggling to appear at home in a foreign tongue.

"Yes, but I want to hear all about everything," Grandma persisted. "Does he like school? Is he keeping well? Has he grown? What did the dear boy have to say?"

"He said a lot of things," replied Mr Jennings "I didn't follow it all, but I gathered that the most important event of the term was when some ozar oik's frog came down to breakfast in his pyjama jacket."

"No, dear, that's wrong," corrected his wife. "The frog was the property of a bogus ruin and it ate stale cake crumbs out of an ink-well behind the boot-lockers."

Grandma's face wore question marks.

"Is that so very important?" she asked.

"Important?" echoed Mr Jennings in tones of mock incredulity. "My dear Grandma, it's more than that. It's – it's super-wizzo-sonic!"

* * *

Half-term passed, and Jennings and Darbishire settled more comfortably into the pattern of school life. Jennings was no genius, but he did his best and managed to hold his own about half-way down the form. Darbishire was a few places higher; his knowledge was slightly better, but it wavered erratically like an aircraft off the beam, and led him to make wild statements with an air of such profound wisdom that the ignorant accepted them as true.

They worked hard for Mr Carter because they liked his

lessons. They worked hard for the Headmaster because they dared not do otherwise, and they worked hard for Mr Wilkins when his manner told them that they had gone quite far enough in the opposite direction. There were other masters on the staff and mistresses too, but they only taught Form Three for occasional lessons, for which they were thankful.

Jennings tried hard to get into the First Eleven. He was hovering on the brink of a place in the side, and when the team was posted on the notice board before each match, he would rush to be the first at the board and scan the list hopefully. But, so far, he had always been disappointed. He knew that if he failed to make the grade this term, he would have to wait a whole year for another chance, for in the Easter Term they played rugger.

Darbishire played football in "D" game, the lowest and the most rabbity of all, and though his boots were no longer tied together, it made no difference to the standard of his play.

In the classroom one evening, some four weeks after half-term, Jennings tackled his friend about it.

"You know, Darbi, your football's pathetic," Jennings told him. "A chap your age shouldn't be playing with Binns minor and all that crush; can't you do something about it?"

"Well, I'm writing an article called *Practical Hints on Positional Play and Advanced Tactics*," was the proud reply. "I asked Mr Carter if he'd put it in the school magazine, and he said he might think about it."

"And who d'you think's going to read it, when they know it's written by a chap who can't even see the ball coming, let alone kick it?"

"That's what Mr Carter said," Darbishire admitted, "so I think it might be better if I used a pen-name, like 'Old Pro,' or 'Wembley Wizard,' or something, don't you think so?"

"H'm," said Jennings, not impressed.

"As a matter of fact," Darbishire went on, "Benedick said he'd rather I wrote something I knew more about for the mag, so I'm thinking of doing a detective story."

"What do you know about detectives?" Jennings asked him.

"Well, anyone can write a detective story," replied Darbishire. "You've only got to think of some characters and a plot, and there you are."

"Yes, I s'pose so," said Jennings, struck by the simplicity of the formula. "But do you think they'd print it? After all, we're not even supposed to read blood and thunders, so I bet they wouldn't print one."

"It needn't be all thud and blunder," replied Darbishire. "We could put some bits of poetry in to make it more highbrow; you know, the hero could quote Shakespeare and stuff, like 'To be or not to be, that is the question.' "

"What is the question?"

"To be or not to be."

"That isn't a question; besides it doesn't make sense. What is to be or not to be?"

"That is the question; I just told you."

"Well, what's the answer?"

"I don't know. It might be anything. It might even be the mystery that the detective's got to solve."

"Oh!"

Detective stories sounded fairly easy, especially if you could put poetry and difficult questions in when you were unable to think of anything else to write.

"How'd it be if I helped you?" said Jennings. "We could write one together. You write Chapter I and I'll do Chapter II, and so on."

"Okay," said Darbishire. "Let's go and start now."

Evening preparation was over and there was half an hour before bedtime, so they took their literary zeal and a notebook down to the tuck-box room and got to work. Darbishire suggested that the library might be a better place in which to woo the muse, but Jennings rejected this on the grounds that it was too quiet and might cramp their style.

"First of all," said Darbishire, licking his pencil, "we've got to think of a name for the detective."

They thought hard for a few moments.

"It ought to be something out of the ordinary," said Jennings.

"Yes, what about Mr Nehemiah Bultitude?"

"Why?"

"Out of the ordinary; or Mr Theophilus Goodbody if you like."

"Oh, don't be daft," said Jennings. "You can't have detectives called things like that. Anybody called Theophilus Goodbody would have to be a clergyman; they always are. And if a chap's a farmer, his name's always Hayseed or Barleycorn, or if he's a schoolmaster he's Dr Whackem or something like that."

They discussed this at length and decided it was obviously a rule to be obeyed.

"You've only got to look in the library," argued Jennings, "and you'll see all Dickens' bods have got names that suit them, like Pecksniff and Cheeryble and Cruncher, and they live at places called Eatanswill."

"But what I can't see," objected Darbishire, "is how anyone knows what they're going to be like before they're born. According to that, if you've got a name like Fuzziwig you could never be as bald as a coot however hard you tried, and if your name's Marlinspike Mainbrace, f'rinstance, you've just got to be a sailor, even if you don't want to be."

"Well, what sort of a name do you have to be born with so's you can be a great detective?"

The work of research went on and yielded the information

that, unless your surname consisted of a single syllable and your parents had been generous enough to give you a two-syllabled first name, you could never hope to succeed in the world of crime detection. Sherlock Holmes, Sexton Blake, Nelson Lee, Dixon Hawke, Falcon Swift, Ferrers Locke – all the best detectives were most careful to have the correct number of syllables to their names.

"Well, what about Egbert Snope?" suggested Darbishire. "That sticks to the rules all right."

"Yes, but it doesn't sound right," objected Jennings. "Pity we don't know any real detectives. We've got a policeman at home," he continued after more thought, "he's not a detective, of course, but he may be one day, and his name's Bill Smithson."

"He can't hope to be much of a detective with a name like that," said Darbishire scornfully, "unless he turns it round and calls himself Billson Smith."

"We want something with more zip, like – I know, what about Flixton Slick?"

"Wizard prang! That'll be super."

"Don't be so wet, Darbi. If a chap was called Wizard Prang he'd be a conjurer, not a detective."

"No, I mean Flixton Slick is wizard prang. I don't mean he is really… I mean, yes, it's a jolly good name."

"All right, then, we'll call the story 'Flixton Slick – Private Investigator.' "

Darbishire moved an amendment that Private Investigator was too cumbersome, and after further debate they decided that Super Sleuth was a more fitting description.

" 'Flixton Slick – Super Sleuth,' "Jennings rolled the syllables round his tongue. "H'm, okay; it's a bit tricky to say, of course; you keep getting 'sloops' in it if you say it too fast."

They decided not to work out the plot before they started.

Darbishire was to write Chapter I, leaving the hero in a difficult situation which Jennings would have to cope with in Chapter II. Thus the story would provide thrills and surprises for author as well as readers right up to the final gripping climax; and the time to start worrying about the gripping climax would not come until the page before was completed.

The dormitory bell rang and the super sleuth was temporarily banished to his Baker Street flat, his dressing-gown and his pipe dreams.

The following day was Friday, and the team to play Bretherton House School the next day appeared on the board at morning break.

Jennings rushed out of class and crashed through the queue. He no longer expected to see his name on the board, but there was always a chance and yes, there it was! He could hardly believe his good fortune. Right-half! Oh, prang! Oh, jolly g! Oh, hefty ziggety door knobs!

"Budge out of the way, Jennings, you're not the only one who wants to see the team."

But Jennings was unable to move. He was held by the magic of his name up there on the board in typewritten capital letters. He walked away in a dream some five minutes later, and then realised that he had been staring at his own name so intently, that he had not the slightest idea of who else had been picked to play, so he had to return to the board and start all over again.

He spent twenty minutes after lunch in cleaning his football boots. He scraped them with a penknife and applied boot polish to soles and uppers, and also to his jacket and trousers, but one could not worry about minor details like that at a time like this.

"There," he said, displaying his handiwork proudly, "how

about those, Bod? I ought to be able to play jolly well tomorrow with my boots as clean as that."

"Well, you are screwy," Temple replied. "You'll get them all muddied up practising this afternoon."

"Gosh, yes!" said Jennings. "I never thought of that. Never mind, I'll do them again this evening."

But, by the evening, he wasn't feeling too well. He had surpassed himself during the practice game and he felt slightly sick at the end of it. He sat quietly through afternoon school, and at tea-time he was unable to eat a thing. This was unheard of, as shepherd's pie was on the menu, and usually Jennings sent his plate up three times; for though custom demanded that one called it muck, yet this was muck with a difference.

"Gosh!" said Venables. "Jennings hasn't had any shepherd's pie. What's the matter, Jen, are you going into training for the match tomorrow?"

"No," he replied, surveying the bread and butter with a jaundiced eye. "No, I just don't feel I want anything to eat; I feel sick."

"Why don't you go to Matron, then?"

"I can't. She'd pack me off to bed, or say I couldn't play or something. I'll be all right in the morning."

Morning dawned, and his inside still felt as though he were descending a sky-scraper in an express lift.

"I'll go and fetch Matron," said Atkinson.

Matron was brisk and hearty, and stood no nonsense. She radiated energy and vigour, and the more ill one felt, the brisker and heartier was Matron. She bounced into the room with a gay snatch of song on her lips, and came to rest before the unwilling invalid.

"Well, well, well," she said. "What's gone wrong here?"

"Well, Matron, I – I feel a bit – umph!" With lightning speed she whipped a thermometer from its case, like a dagger from its sheath, and plunged it between her patient's teeth before he could finish his sentence.

"Right as rain yesterday," Matron carolled blithely. "Can't have you being a death's-head at the feast like this."

"Well, Matron, I – "

"Quiet, quiet. Never talk with a thermom. in your mouth. Now, then, you others" – she turned to the rest of the dormitory who were clustered round the bed like flies round a honey-pot – "off you go. The breakfast bell will be going in two shakes of a lamb's tail."

She hummed contentedly for a minute, took the thermometer from Jennings' mouth, and narrowed her eyes to see the fine column of mercury.

"We'll soon have you up and about again," she said brightly. "No, no, no, not yet awhile," she continued, as Jennings started to get out of bed. She diagnosed a bilious attack and sentenced him to stay where he was for the morning.

"But I'll be all right for the match this afternoon, won't I, Matron?"

"Match this afternoon? Good gracious, no! Quite out of the question."

"Oh, but, Matron, please, I must – "

"I may let you up for a bit this afternoon; you can sit on the couch in my sitting-room, but no football; rigidly taboo."

This was a catastrophe; this was the end of everything. After weeks of effort, he had worked and played and willed his way into the team only to spend the day of the match in bed. It was a morning darkened by the fog of despair.

After a light lunch, Matron allowed him to come to her sitting-room.

"Rise and shine," she sang as she bustled into the dormitory. "We'll have you as right as a trivet by tomorrow."

"But it's no good being all right tomorrow," Jennings lamented. "It doesn't matter how ill I am then; it's today. And they'll go and play Johnson in my place; I bet they do."

"Very nice for Johnson," said Matron. "It's an ill wind that blows nobody any good. And after the match, I've promised Darbishire he can come up to my sitting-room and talk to you. That will be nice and cheery, won't it?"

Darbishire's conversation sounded a poor substitute for playing in the match, and Jennings spent a nerve-racked afternoon. He could hear the cheering on the football pitch, but he could see nothing, and it was infuriating to listen to cheers and not to know what they portended.

Darbishire arrived after the match, and Jennings demanded details.

"We won," said Darbishire. "One nil, and Johnson scored the goal; he played a super game. Everyone said how good he was, and he'll probably stay in the team now."

He chatted on, unconsciously rubbing salt into the wound.

"It's just as well for the school that you were ill, 'cos Johnson wouldn't have been playing otherwise, and then we shouldn't have scored."

It does nothing to soothe the nerves of a convalescent to tell him that his suffering is a blessing to the community, and Jennings was anything but pleased with the heavy-handed attempts to cheer him up. So when Darbishire proudly announced that he had brought Chapter I of "Flixton Slick – Super Sleuth" with him, Jennings' mood of criticism was hostile.

"All right, chuck it over," he said. "I don't suppose it's much good, but I might as well read it." Darbishire handed over the notebook reverently and sat back with the smile of the author who knows that praise is on its way.

Jennings read aloud: " '*Chapter I. A vast crowd had gathered at the airfield to see Flixton Slick – Super Sleuth – take off the wings of his aeroplane...*' What's he want to take the wings off for?" he demanded.

"It doesn't say that," said Darbishire. "There should be a full stop after take off. They'd come to see him take off. Full stop."

"Oh, I see," said Jennings. " '*The wings of his aeroplane glistened in the sun. How the vast crowd did cheer as the aeroplane was airborne and waved handkerchiefs...*' " He broke off. "That's daft," he said. "How can an aeroplane wave handkerchiefs? You might as well make it flap its wings."

"No, you goof," said the author. "I mean the crowd waved handkerchiefs."

"Well, why don't you say what you mean?"

He was certainly not going to be kind to the masterpiece after listening to Darbishire's praise of Johnson.

"Oh, go on," said Darbishire. "You know perfectly well what it means."

" '*It was not a very exiting journey...*' " He stopped again. "Well, of course it wasn't," he said. "You don't keep making exits from an aeroplane like you do when you're playing 'Henry V' and things."

"I don't know what you're talking about," said Darbishire.

Jennings showed him the passage.

"That's supposed to be *exciting* not exit-ing," the author explained. "I don't think you're trying. Read properly."

Jennings clicked his tongue reproachfully.

" '*Soon Flixton Slick arrived at Scotland Yard...*' " he read. " '*He had been sent for to investigate a mysterious spy who was working for a foreign power. His nickname was the Silent Shadow and his real name was only whispered...*' Was he a Red Indian, then?" Jennings demanded, breaking off.

"No, why?"

"They have names like *Sitting Bull* and *Laughing Mountain*, so I thought *Only Whispered* might be a name like that."

"Oh, you are a ruin," exclaimed the author in some distress. "Go on. His real name was only whispered *because…* and then it goes on."

"Oh, yes '*…because it might cause embarrassment to a member of the cabinet called Sir James, who was a Minister without Portfolio.*' "

"That means he hadn't got one of those despatch case things," the author explained.

"Why hadn't he?"

"Well, if you read on, you'll see. He'd had his portfolio stolen by the Silent Shadow with the secret plans in."

"Oh, I see. '*Sir James was at Scotland Yard telling the chief of Police about this when Flixton Slick arrived, and while the Chief of Police told him all about it, Sir James remained without.*' Does that mean he remained outside, or remained without portfolio?" the critic inquired.

"Well, both, really. It doesn't matter which way you take it. Go on! It's good, isn't it?"

" '*The Chief of Police told Flixton Slick that the Silent Shadow's headquarters were in this warehouse that I shall tell you about later, so Flixton Slick left Scotland Yard with three uninformed constables…*' " Jennings stopped again to inquire what it was they had not been informed about.

"You can't read properly," objected Darbishire, "you're spoiling it. It doesn't say anything about their not being informed."

"Well, what's this, then?" demanded Jennings, passing the exercise book back to the author.

"Oh, sorry, yes, I made a slip. It's meant to be *uniformed*. Look, would you like me to read it to you; you don't seem to be doing it very well."

"It doesn't make sense whoever reads it, as far as I can see," Jennings grumbled.

Darbishire's pride was shattered by this time, but he made a last attempt to silence the hostile criticism.

"Well, this bit that's coming's ever so exciting," he said. "Listen; I'll read it this time. '*So Flixton Slick left Scotland Yard with three uniformed constables and went to the warehouse. He burst in. The Silent Shadow was hiding in a corner with the portfolio belonging to the Minister without Portfolio on a table in front of him. When he saw Flixton Slick he whipped out a revolver. Crack! Crack! Crack! Three shots rang out. Two policemen fell dead and the third whistled through his hat –*' "

"Wait a minute," Jennings interrupted. "The third did what?"

"Whistled through his hat."

"He must have been crazy."

"Who? The Silent Shadow? Yes, he was really, you see – "

"No, the other policeman. If two of your friends got shot dead you might take off your hat as a mark of respect, but you wouldn't whistle through it. Besides, they wear helmets, not hats."

"It doesn't mean the policeman whistled through his hat, you ozard oik." Darbishire became red in the face with anger at this further attempt to deride his masterpiece. "It means the third bullet whistled through Slixton Flick's hat."

"You can't even get the name right now. Slixton Flick – Slooper-Sooth," Jennings jeered.

Darbishire hurled the book at him, but missed by several feet.

"Rotten shot!" said Jennings. "It wasn't even near enough to whistle through my hat, even if I'd had one."

"You're being ozard squared beastly on purpose," Darbishire shouted. "I've a jolly good mind not to be friends with you any more. My father says – "

131

"Go on then, don't be," Jennings called back, just as loudly. "And I don't care what your father says either. You come in here to cheer me up, and tell me what a marvellous player Johnson is, and what a good thing it is that I'm too ill to play."

"Well, there was no need for you to be all stupid about Flixton Slick when you knew all the time, really… And I'm jolly well going to cross you off my Revised Cake List, so that'll show you."

They were both shouting; Darbishire nearly in tears, and Jennings angry and miserable.

The door opened and Matron bounced in to find out the cause of the uproar.

"Now, now, now," she said. "Come, come, come. What's this? What's this? I leave you as thick as thieves and, hey presto, I come back to find you going for each other hammer and tongs."

Jennings wondered why on earth Matron always had to talk like that. Normally, he enjoyed her conversation but, in his present mood, her hearty banter annoyed him.

"Off you go then, Darbishire," she said.

Darbishire departed, muttering darkly about severed friendships.

"And I shan't let you invite friends into my sitting-room," Matron went on, "if you're going to start a rough and tumble as soon as my back's turned."

"No, Matron," said Jennings.

"And you'd better go down into school after tea; you seem hale and hearty enough."

"Yes, Matron."

She went out, leaving Jennings alone with the bitterness of his thoughts. He'd had a bad day, and a small wave of self-pity splashed over him. What a rotter Darbishire was! What an out-and-out cad! He was glad he had seen through him.

Fancy bursting in on an invalid, in a delicate state of health, and shattering his nerves to pieces with blood and thunder stories of missing portfolios. It was enough to have given him a relapse. And more important still – but, no, he couldn't bring himself to think about the match.

He was still trying hard not to think about the match when Mr Carter looked in.

"Hallo, Jennings," he said. "Pity you had to miss the match. Very good game it was, too. Johnson played well," he added, unnecessarily.

"Yes, I know, sir. I was awfully fed up about it. I don't s'pose I'll get another chance now."

"But of course you will," said Mr Carter; "next Saturday."

"Oh, is there a match next Saturday? Coo, wizard prang!"

"We're playing Bracebridge School," Mr Carter told him.

"Mm, yes, but now Johnson's turned out to be so jolly good, I don't s'pose I'll get a look in."

"Yes, you will. I'm going to play you and Johnson next time, and drop somebody else from the forward line."

The grey mist of gloom which had lain heavily over Jennings' spirits suddenly cleared.

"Oh, super-duper-sonic, sir," he said. "Thanks most awfully, sir. Gosh, I'm looking forward to next Saturday!"

He was feeling fine when he went downstairs, and the first person he saw was a dejected and miserable Darbishire. He was standing by a waste-paper basket in the common-room, tearing his deathless prose manuscript into little strips. And, as each scrap of paper fell into the basket, it was as though another link had been severed in the chain of their friendship.

"Poor Darbi," thought Jennings, eyeing him through the rose-coloured spectacles that his place in the team had lent him; he had misjudged Darbishire. What a wizard decent cove he was really! His mood of happiness was so strong, that it wiped out the resentment that he had felt earlier on.

"Hallo, Darbi, old fellow," he called from the doorway.

Darbishire looked up disgustedly.

"Oh, it's you, is it?" he said. "Well, jolly well go away; I've finished with you." And he tore the last page into sixteen small pieces.

"Now, look here, Darbi," said Jennings. "I'm terribly sorry I was so ozard about your story; I thought it was jolly g, really."

Darbishire looked up suspiciously, hoping, but not expecting, to find an olive branch within reach.

"Are you pulling my leg?" he asked.

"No, honestly. But I wasn't feeling quite myself after the match. I was something – what d'you call it – like effervescent?"

"Convalescent?"

"Yes, but I'm all right now."

"Well, of course, if it comes to that," Darbishire said, "I s'pose I can be said to have ridden roughshod over your feelings about not playing."

"Oh, forget it," said Jennings. "Tell you what, let's write 'Flixton Slick' out again. I'll do it if you like."

"Okay," said Darbishire, thawing visibly. "You – you..." He was proud of Chapter I, and there lingered in his mind the nagging thought that Jennings was seeking a further opportunity to mock his literary efforts.

"What?" said Jennings.

"You do really like Chapter I, don't you; as far as you got, anyway?"

"Of course I do. It's first rate. Nearly as good as *Treasure Island*. Come on, you dictate and I'll write."

Armed with a new notebook they went to the tuck-box room.

Darbishire felt important now that he was about to dictate. He had never had a secretary before. He cleared his throat.

" 'A vast crowd had gathered at the airfield to see Flixton Slick take off. Full stop.' "

The rift had been healed.

9

Mr Wilkins Has an Idea

On Monday Jennings wrote in his diary, "*Only five days to the match or four if you do not count today or Saturday morning.*"

On Tuesday he wrote, "*Only four days more or three not counting today and Sat.*" And those with a bent for mathematics can work out the diarist's entries for the remainder of the week. By Friday morning, when only one day remained – or none, if you counted the other way – Jennings' excitement was beginning to interfere with his work.

Mr Wilkins didn't like Fridays. He had to take Form Three for two lessons before the break and again immediately afterwards. Halfway through the second lesson Mr Wilkins began to send out tremors indicating that an earthquake might be expected at short notice. Form Three regarded this as a promising sign; it meant that the rest of the morning would teem with interest; always provided, of course, that someone else received the brunt of the attack.

Mr Wilkins strode between the desks, peering critically at the geometrical figures that the boys were copying from the board. When he arrived at Jennings' desk, he stopped and a look of anguish clouded his features.

"My goodness," he said, "what d'you call those?"

"Those are incongruous triangles, sir," Jennings explained.

"They certainly are," said Mr Wilkins; "but they're not meant to be. You can't draw congruent triangles with sprawling lines like that. Look at them; they ought to be thin, and these lines are as thick as – well, I don't know what!"

"As thick as thieves, sir?" prompted Darbishire.

"It's my pencil, sir," explained Jennings; "it hasn't got much of a point."

"Neither has your compass," complained Mr Wilkins, examining the contents of the geometry box. "What have you been doing; playing darts with it? Just look at this ruler, and this protractor!"

They were, indeed, a sorry-looking collection of instruments. The ruler was warped and chipped, for one cannot fight rapier duels without damaging one's weapon. There were intricate carvings, too, which suggested that the ruler had been used as an Indian totem pole; and though it might have passed muster as a bread knife, it was no longer a reliable instrument for drawing straight lines. There was a piece missing from the protractor – a neat rectangle of celluloid which Jennings had removed in order to make a windscreen for his miniature motorcar; and the point of his compass had done duty for so many tasks requiring a sharp point, that it was bent like a fish-hook.

"How on earth do you expect to draw straight lines and accurate angles with this junk?" fumed Mr Wilkins. "Look at this figure you've drawn here; what's it meant to be?"

"Two parallel lines with a thingummy going across, sir."

"Yes, but look at the shape; look at this angle; what sort of an angle is it?"

Jennings regarded it dubiously.

"Well, sir, it's a little difficult to say, but I think it's meant to be an alternate angle, sir."

"You *think*!" boomed Mr Wilkins. "You *think* it's meant to be alternate! Well, don't think; you're not meant to think; you're meant to know."

"Yes, sir," said Jennings.

"And if it is an alternate angle," continued Mr Wilkins, giving the wavering lines the benefit of the doubt, "it must be alternate to another one. Now, then, which angle is it alternate to?"

Jennings surveyed the maze of thick lines helplessly.

"I don't know, sir," he confessed.

"You don't know!" echoed Mr Wilkins. "Well, think, you silly little boy, think!"

"But you just told me not to think, sir. You said I wasn't meant to think."

The class rocked with laughter. They went on laughing long after the joke had ceased to be funny. They forced themselves to go on laughing because a joke, even though it is a bad one, is a signal for a laugh, and the longer it can be kept up the better.

But Mr Wilkins did not laugh. They were laughing at him, and not with him, and nobody enjoys that.

"Quiet," he ordered.

The laughter died away slowly and then the comments started.

"Sir, Jennings was quite right, sir, you did tell him he wasn't meant to think; didn't you, sir?"

"Sir, you meant he should think and then, when he's thought, he shouldn't have to think any more; didn't you, sir?"

"But, sir, if you tell him to think one minute, and then the next minute you tell him not to – "

"Silence," thundered Mr Wilkins. "Sit up and fold your arms, all of you."

By the loudness of his voice and the fury in his eye, the class was silenced. But it was the shallow silence of necessity and not the deep silence of respect. They stopped talking but took delight in pretending to be frightened by the violence of Mr Wilkins' anger. They sought shelter behind exercise books, and quaked with exaggerated grimaces of terror. They raised their coat collars about their ears and crouched low in their seats as the imaginary blast whistled fearfully above their heads.

"The next boy who makes a sound will be…" threatened Mr Wilkins; he could think of no punishment drastic enough. "…Well, he'd better look out," he finished lamely.

The class could distinguish between bark and bite. They were silent, but they smiled and they looked at one another with the sort of expression that Mr Wilkins found far more infuriating than speech. Everything had been all right, he told himself, until that fatal burst of laughter. Now they were out of hand, and the angrier he became, the funnier they thought it was. True, they were quiet, but if Mr Carter or the Headmaster were in charge, it would be a different sort of quietness. What should he do? He could keep them in, of course, but they didn't seem to mind that. What he needed was a punishment that would really make them sit up. Something so drastic that it would command instant respect for evermore. He was still trying to think of a suitable punishment when the bell rang for break, and he dismissed the class.

Jennings raced downstairs to the notice board. Yes, there it was. "First Eleven versus Bracebridge School"; and there was his name in the forward line. Johnson, as befitted the star discovery of the previous week, was playing right-half, but Bromwich major had been dropped and Jennings was playing inside-right. He feasted his eyes on the typewritten inscription and checked his name twice for spelling mistakes. All was in order, and he rushed off to find Darbishire.

Darbishire was still in the classroom with his exercise

book open on the desk before him. He was studying a gaily coloured booklet issued by a shipping company, which set out, in extravagant terms, the delights in store for anyone who booked a passage to Australia in one of their liners.

"Come and look at the board, Darbi," called Jennings. "The team's up; I'm playing inside-right."

"Good," said Darbishire, and went on studying the booklet.

"But don't you want to see it?" asked Jennings, unable to believe that anyone could resist the temptation of seeing it with their own eyes.

"I believe you," said Darbishire. "No point in going down and reading what you've already told me."

"Oh," said Jennings. "I'm glad I'm playing, aren't you?"

"Yes," replied Darbishire, intent on his ocean-going research.

"Inside-right, I'm playing," said Jennings.

"I know, you've just told me."

"Bromo has been dropped, and I'm playing inside-right."

"That's the fifty millionth time you've told me that in two seconds," said Darbishire. "You're playing inside-right. Okay, I know now. If anyone asks me if I know where you're playing, I'll say, 'Yes, inside-right.' I don't s'pose anyone will, but if they do, I'll have the answer off pat. 'Inside-right,' I'll say." There was meant to be subtle irony and reproach against swanking in Darbishire's remark, but it was wasted on Jennings.

"Yes, inside-right," Jennings said. "Don't forget. If anyone asks you, just say I'm playing inside-right."

"I'll put it up on the blackboard if you like," Darbishire replied, and his tone was heavy with sarcasm.

"I shouldn't bother," said Jennings, "you'll remember anyway."

Darbishire returned to his study of the Antipodes.

"What are you doing?" asked Jennings.

"Well, I haven't done my geog. prep. and Wilkie's taking us next lesson."

"Gosh, neither have I," said Jennings. "What is it, anyway?"

"Wheat farming in Australia," replied Darbishire. "Mind you, I'm not going to make a habit of working during break," he went on. "I mean, that sort of thing leads to nervous breakdowns and brainstorms and things, but judging from what old Wilkie was like last lesson, I think it would be as well if we got our prep. done."

"Think there'll be a hoo-hah if we haven't?"

"Yes, I do. A supersonic hoo-hah cubed."

Reluctantly Jennings went to his desk and took out his geography book.

"What goes on in Australia?" he asked.

"Rabbits," replied Darbishire. "Millions and millions of them; they're a pest, and they eat all the wheat that the farmers spend their time trying to grow."

"Well, that'll do for a start, anyway," Jennings said. "Now shut up talking, I'm going to write my essay." He retired to the mental realms of scholarship and wrote. His crossed nib splayed widely apart on his down-strokes and clicked scratchily, sending out thin showers of inky vapour on every up-stroke of the pen.

Darbishire wore a puzzled frown as he studied his travel booklet. It described the splendour of Australia in glowing terms; the sunsets, the climate, the grandeur of the scenery were painted in the richest colours, for the author's intention was to put his readers in holiday mood, and not to worry about the mundane tasks of making a living by toil and soil. Darbishire sighed; still the chap ought to know what he was writing about, so he started to copy the opening paragraph into his exercise book.

"It ought to please old Wilkie, anyhow," he thought.

Unaware of this treat in store, Mr Wilkins paced his sitting-room like a caged lion; he had got to do something to show those boys that he was a force to be reckoned with. But what? He had already dismissed the commonplace punishments as being ineffective and, in twenty minutes, he would have to face the form again. He ceased his pacing and went upstairs to consult Mr Carter.

The door of Mr Carter's study quivered under the assault of Mr Wilkins' knock; the handle rattled like a burst of machine gun fire, and the papers on the desk fluttered in the breeze as the door was flung wide.

"Really, Wilkins," Mr Carter protested. "Must you always come into my room like a herd of buffalo stampeding across the prairie?"

"You'd be feeling a bit frantic if you'd just had Form Three for two lessons running," came the answer. "I tell you, Carter, that form's turning my hair grey. Can't behave; will talk; won't work; must fidget. I've been shouting myself hoarse in there all morning."

"That's probably the trouble," Mr Carter replied. "Have you ever tried talking quietly? You see, Wilkins, if you rampage round a classroom like a bull in a china shop, they just think it's most frightfully funny."

"Nonsense," barked Mr Wilkins. "I've got to make myself felt. The trouble is, I'm too easy with them. I tell you, Carter, I haven't got enough authority in this school. I wish I were the Headmaster; I'd soon see things were done properly."

"I doubt it," replied Mr Carter. "It's not so easy being a Headmaster as you might think."

"Nonsense," Mr Wilkins dismissed the difficulties with a wave of his hand which knocked a brass ashtray off the mantelpiece. "Sorry, old man," he said, retrieving it. "What was I saying?"

"You were saying that a Headmaster's job was a bed of roses."

"So it is," said Mr Wilkins. "There's nothing in it. Why, if I were in charge, I could run this school with my eyes shut."

"Yes," agreed Mr Carter, "that's just about how you would run it; both eyes so tightly shut, that you wouldn't know what was going on."

"I – I – well, you know what I mean." Mr Wilkins felt he wasn't getting the sympathy he deserved. "It's all very well for you," he went on, "they do as you tell them without any funny answers. You don't even have to shout at them; you just give them a look and they eat out of your hand. I wish I could do it."

"Well, for a start, try talking quietly and don't move around like a bulldozer dancing the Highland fling."

"You're not much help, are you?" Mr Wilkins said. "I thought you might be able to suggest a suitable punishment for the next time they try to be funny."

"You could give them a detention," suggested Mr Carter.

"That's not enough by itself," Mr Wilkins vetoed the idea. "I've done that before. No, I want something that'll make them see they can't play fast and loose in my lessons and, by jove, when I've thought of something, that form's going to get it in the neck."

The telephone on Mr Carter's desk rang.

"Excuse me," he said, and picked up the receiver. "Hallo! Linbury Court School... Yes, Carter speaking... Oh, hallo, Parkinson, how are you?... Are you bringing a strong team over tomorrow?"

The voice at the other end of the wire said that it was sorry, but that it wouldn't be bringing a team over at all. German measles had claimed a victim at Bracebridge School some time earlier, and though the patient had now recovered, the school's month of quarantine would not expire until the following week. Mr Parkinson apologised profusely for forgetting to let Mr Carter know earlier, but there it was. It was too near the end of the term to arrange another game, so they would have to regard the fixture as cancelled.

Mr Carter replaced the receiver and relayed the news.

"Oh, pity," said Mr Wilkins. "I was looking forward to seeing that match tomorrow; should have been a good game. The boys will be disappointed." Already his old enemy, the kind heart, had switched his feelings from wrath at the boys' misdeeds to sympathy at their being deprived of a match.

"Jennings will be upset," he went on. "Keen as mustard, and a jolly good little player he is, too. Still, if the game's scratched…" He broke off, as the Idea flashed into his mind. The Idea took root and grew, spreading its branches and flowering profusely in every corner of his mind until he was almost dazzled with its brilliance.

"Good heavens, yes," he murmured ecstatically. "Why not? It's just what I've been waiting for."

"What is?" inquired Mr Carter.

"Now I've got Form Three where I want them! Any more nonsense from them and I'll cancel the match against Bracebridge tomorrow."

Mr Carter sighed, and he spoke with the patience normally reserved for explaining the nicer points of English grammar to lower forms.

"But it's cancelled already," he said gently. "I've just told you. They're in quarantine for German measles."

"Yes, yes, yes," Mr Wilkins broke in impatiently. "I know that; you know that. But the boys don't know it. It's the very weapon I wanted. The first bit of trouble I get, I can say, 'Right. The whole lot of you can stay in tomorrow, and there'll be no match.' Just like that, see?"

Mr Wilkins was delighted with his Idea. If they thought he

had the power to cancel football matches, they would eye him with a new respect; and when they saw that he actually put this terrible threat into execution, there wouldn't be any more funny answers during his lessons.

Mr Carter was shocked.

"You can't do that!" he protested. "It's making out that you've got the authority to do things which you can't do. Why, even the Head would think twice before cancelling a match as a punishment."

"But I'm not really cancelling it; that's done already. I'm just pretending to."

Mr Wilkins stuck to his Idea. He argued that his mild deception would be a good thing for his discipline, and would make no difference whatever to the existing state of affairs. If the match had to be cancelled, why shouldn't he use it to his advantage?

"But it's not cricket," objected Mr Carter. "Yes, but don't you see, Carter, that I'm being most frightfully lenient; why, I shan't be punishing them at all, really, if they can't play tomorrow, anyway."

"I don't like the idea," Mr Carter muttered. "It's – it's – unscrupulous. Besides, they might all behave so well that you don't want to punish them."

Mr Wilkins thought this remark was very funny. He laughed long and loud at such a fantastic idea, and he was still laughing some minutes later when the bell rang.

"Ah," he said. "Now I'm going on the war-path with a vengeance, and I'm going into Form Three looking for trouble."

"I don't like it," repeated Mr Carter, as Mr Wilkins stalked towards the door with a determined look in his eye.

Mr Carter clutched the papers on his desk. He said: "Don't slam the – "

The door slammed loudly behind Mr Wilkins.

In the classroom, Form Three opened their books for the next lesson.

"It's geog. with Wilkie," said Venables. "He'll probably be in a super bate. I did a rotten essay."

"Never mind," said Jennings. "Bracebridge match tomorrow; I'm playing inside-right." He practised some imaginary shots at goal with vocal accompaniment. "Wham!... Pheeew!... Doyng!... Goal!..." He shook hands with himself and bowed left and right.

"Don't swank," said Temple.

"Well, I'm better than you, Bod," Jennings replied. "I must be 'cos I've seen Manchester United play in a cup tie; I stick up for Manchester; I shall probably play for them when I grow up."

"I bet!" jeered Atkinson.

"Only every other Saturday, of course," Jennings amended, " 'cos I'll be playing rugger for the Harlequins the other times."

"Why do you stick up for Manchester?" inquired Temple. "I bet you've never even been there."

"Well – no," Jennings agreed; "but I've got a good reason to stick up for them, 'cos my godmother lives in Liverpool and they're joined by a canal, so that almost makes me a Manchesterian, doesn't it?"

"If it comes to that," Darbishire put in, "my mother's got a carpet sweeper called the Northampton cleaner, so that means I'm entitled to stick up for Northampton Town."

"Shut up, Darbishire," said Temple, "nobody asked you."

Heavy footsteps could be heard approaching along the corridor; there was never any need for a lookout when Mr Wilkins was due to take a lesson.

"Get our your geography prep.," he called, while still some five yards from the classroom door. There was a note of confidence in his voice, but it passed unheeded in Form Three.

Venables put up his hand as Mr Wilkins took his seat.

"Did we have to write our prep. in our books, sir?" he asked.

"Where else would you expect to write it; on the ceiling?"

"No, sir. I mean, I wondered whether we just had to learn about Australia and not write an essay."

Mr Wilkins glared.

"So you haven't written an essay, eh? Very well, then, if you're looking for trouble – "

"Oh, but, sir, I have written one."

"You said you hadn't."

"No, sir. I just wondered, that was all."

"Don't talk nonsense," said Mr Wilkins. He called Jennings up to the master's desk and inspected his efforts. " 'In Austeralia,' " he read aloud, " *'there is wheat but the rabits are a pest like rats so the farmers get very cross because the rabits eat the wheat in England rabits are not a pest you can have chinchla and angora mine was white with some brown fur on and his name was Bobtail and so I got a tea chest and put straw down and made a hutch…'* " Mr Wilkins stopped reading "Of all the muddle-headed bone-heads–!" Words failed him for a moment. "What d'you mean by serving me up with nonsense like this?"

"But, sir, it's not nonsense," Jennings protested "It's true. My rabbit was brown and white; m'uncle gave him to me for my birthday."

"But I set an essay on Australian wheat growing not the life story of some wretched rodent!"

"Bobtail his name was," Jennings corrected.

"I don't care if his name was Moses," Mr Wilkins expostulated. "It's not the point; it's not geography; it's – it's not – "

"My father would say it was 'not germane to the issue,' sir," Darbishire put in helpfully.

"That's enough, Darbishire." Mr Wilkins turned back to the rabbit fancier. "You illiterate nitwit, Jennings, can't you see that your essay's miles away from the subject? It's a perfect example of – er – of – "

"Juvenile delinquency, sir?" suggested Darbishire.

"Be quiet, Darbishire." Mr Wilkins turned on him angrily.

"Sorry, sir," Darbishire said meekly.

"The trouble with you, Jennings, is that you're half-asleep. You need waking up. Go and put your head under the tap in the wash-room and see if that'll clear your brain at all."

"What, now, sir?" Jennings asked.

"Yes, now, and perhaps you'll come back a bit brighter. Go along."

Jennings departed to the wash-room, and Mr Wilkins called Darbishire up to his desk and began to read his essay. He read, " '*The grandiose splendours of the Australian countryside unfold a never-to-be-forgotten scenic pageant that remains a priceless jewel in the memory for all time. Fair and fragrant is the vast undulation of the plains stretching relentlessly to the horizon, where in the declining rays of the setting sun, the eye of the observer is entranced to behold…*' " Mr Wilkins looked up, but, unlike the observer, his eye was not entranced with what it beheld. "I suppose you're going to tell me that this is all your own work?" he said.

"Well, no, not entirely," Darbishire confessed; "but I went to a lot of trouble and did research and stuff, sir."

"And what about the wheat growing?"

"Oh, that comes later," Darbishire explained. "Much later actually; in fact, I haven't quite got up to writing it yet. All this early part is just to put the reader in the right mood, sir."

"It's putting me in a mood, Darbishire," Mr Wilkins admitted; "but it's not by any means the sort of mood you're aiming at."

The door opened and Jennings appeared. His visit to the wash-room had made him brighter of eye, but his head bore no signs of immersion. Mr Wilkins looked at him narrowly. This was deliberate disobedience. Very well, he was ready to meet it.

"You've been very quick, Jennings," he said, with studied calmness. "Come here."

Jennings came.

"Did you put your head under the tap as I told you?"

"Yes, sir."

Mr Wilkins produced his ace.

"Then do you mind telling me," he inquired patiently, "do you mind explaining why your hair is quite dry?"

"Well, sir, you never told me to turn the tap on." For the second time that morning the class rocked with laughter. Natural hearty laughter to start with, but, after a while, this was exhausted and they had to fall back on pantomime. The genuine laughter of schoolboys doesn't take the form of knee-smiting and thigh-slapping, but in their efforts to give the impression that their mirth was uncontrollable, they rolled about in their seats and smote their knees and slapped their thighs; then they smote their neighbours' knees and slapped their neighbours' thighs, and gave each other coy and playful pushes – anything to focus the spotlight of attention upon their counterfeit glee. Speech came through tears of merriment.

"Oh, sir, isn't Jennings smashing! Jolly g. answer, wasn't it, sir?"

"You asked for that one, sir. A real priority prang!"

"He was more awake than you thought, wasn't he, sir?"

149

"Sir, you should have told him to turn the tap on, sir."

"Sir, did you forget to tell him to turn the tap on, sir, because if you didn't actually tell him to turn the tap on, sir, he wouldn't know he had to, would he, sir?"

Mr Wilkins waited – grimly, quietly patient. He could afford to wait, for very soon the tables would be turned. Silence came at last, and Mr Wilkins spoke in tones unusually quiet for a person of his forceful nature.

"I've never in all my life," he began, "heard such a deplorable exhibition of hooliganism. If that is your idea of being clever, Jennings – "

"But it was only what you told him to do, sir," put in Venables.

"...as the rest of the form obviously appreciates this cheap type of humour, they will have to suffer for it. The whole class will come in for two hours detention tomorrow afternoon."

"Oh, sir!" said the whole class.

Temple put up his hand.

"Sir, you can't keep us in tomorrow, sir," he said, "because of the match, and even if we're not in the team, we have to watch it, sir; the Head said so."

"Yes, sir, the Bracebridge match, sir," echoed three other boys anxious to share in the propagation of the news.

The class exchanged superior smiles; knowing glances that plainly said that that had cooked Mr Wilkins' goose for him. They waited for him to retract his rash statement; but Mr Wilkins paused just long enough to secure the right effect, and then he pounced.

"You will not be playing Bracebridge School tomorrow," he announced. "You can consider the match cancelled."

The form was incredulous. Had Mr Wilkins some new powers that they had not been informed of? That was hardly playing the game.

"Oh, but, sir," they expostulated, "you can't do that, sir; really, you can't, sir."

"You heard what I said," Mr Wilkins repeated gravely. "I warned you and you took no notice. Very well, then – no match."

"Oh, sir," said the class, stunned and resentful, but forced now to believe the terrible news.

Darbishire intervened with a policy of appeasement.

"Supposing we behave most frightfully decently from now on, sir, won't you let us off?"

"I'm not prepared to argue; the match is cancelled," repeated Mr Wilkins in tones of finality. He had been careful not to state, in so many words, that he, personally, was responsible for the cancellation; but if they had formed that impression, he was certainly not going to disillusion them.

As the awful consequence of their behaviour spread through the minds of the class, their resentment was switched from Mr Wilkins to the cause of the trouble and, in a matter of seconds, Jennings ceased to be the hero and became the villain of the piece.

"Jen-nings!" they jeered derisively, united in venom against the new foe.

"You are a fool, Jennings!"

"Yes, you pestilent oik. You did it on purpose. Why couldn't you behave decently and do what Mr Wilkins told you?" Venables, whose hearty laughter had been a feature of the uproar barely a minute before, now sounded shocked that anyone could have been guilty of a joke in such bad taste.

"Well, you thought it was funny, anyway," Jennings said.

"I never thought it was funny," Venables replied in tones of outraged innocence. "I thought it was just too putrid for words."

"So did I," put in Temple. "It *would* be Jennings to get the match cancelled!"

Jennings tried to defend himself, but the odds were against him. The form wanted a scapegoat, and he was the obvious choice.

Mr Wilkins allowed the criticism to run its course. He was above it all; an aloof figure who made decrees of world-shattering importance. "Well, they asked for it," he told his protesting conscience. Aloud he said, "And now, perhaps, we can resume the lesson."

"Sir," said Jennings, "it was all my fault, sir. Can I do the detention and you let the others off so they can have the match, sir?"

"No, Jennings."

"But, sir, it's not fair to them," he protested miserably. "Please let them have the match, sir, and I'll stay in even though" – he could hardly bring himself to utter the dread words – "even though it means I can't play. And – and I'll go back and get my head wet, too, sir," he added generously.

Mr Wilkins cast a disdainful glance at the author of the funny answer and, for a moment, the sight of the pathetic, troubled expression, made him relent. But only for a moment. He steeled himself and spoke in tones of simple dignity.

"I'm not in the habit of having my decisions questioned by insignificant little boys," he said. "And now, Darbishire, we will continue to read your essay."

Form Three sat in dejected silence, stunned and numb, and there was a song in Mr Wilkins' heart as he picked up Darbishire's exercise book and turned his attention to the scenic splendours of the Antipodes.

10

The Poisonous Spider

The news travelled fast, and by lunch-time it had spread all over the school. "Old Wilkie's cancelled the match tomorrow, and all because of Jennings." The grim tidings passed from mouth to mouth and little pieces were added on and facts were twisted round.

"I say, have you heard? Old Wilkie's cancelled the Bracebridge match."

"He can't do that!"

"Can't he? He's done it, and all because of Jennings; he told him to put his head under the tap."

"Gosh, did you hear that? Jennings told Wilkie to go and stick his head under a tap. No wonder Wilkie got mad."

Jennings' name was Mud throughout lunch, and he had little appetite for the meal. He knew he was largely to blame for Mr Wilkins' decision, but it seemed unfair to him that those who laughed the loudest when all was well, should now be the loudest in their condemnation. Only Darbishire remained faithful, and after lunch he slipped away from the anti-Jennings protest meeting which was going on in the common-room, and went in search of his friend. He found him brooding darkly behind the boot-lockers.

"Never mind, Jennings," said Darbishire. "Can't be helped; and I don't think it was your fault, really, 'cos if they hadn't laughed like that, old Wilkie wouldn't have go in such a bate. My father says that – "

"Wilkie's a mean cad," said Jennings. "He's as ozard as a coot."

"You can't say that," objected the knowledgeable Darbishire. "You can only be as bald as a coot."

"Who can?"

"Anyone; it's a simile," the pedant explained. "What you meant was, either Wilkie is as bald as a coot – "

"I never said he was bald," Jennings objected.

"No, but if you wanted to."

"Why should I want to say he was bald if he isn't? I said he was ozard, that's all."

"Of course," mused Darbishire, "I s'pose you could make up a simile and say he was as ozard as a buzzard. My father says that the history of the English language – "

Jennings was in no mood to listen to a lecture on the origins of language.

"Come on," he said. "Let's go."

"Where?"

"Anywhere; I couldn't care less."

Aimlessly they slouched across the main hall, where their gaze was affronted by the team list for Saturday's match, hanging limply by its drawing pin, and across the sheet of paper was the word "Cancelled" in bold block capitals of red ink. Vaguely they wandered across the quad, and round the corner to the yard behind the kitchen where tradesmen's vans unloaded laundry and meat and groceries. Old Pyjams was there, opening a crate with hammer and pliers.

"I bet you I know what's for tea," Jennings said. "I bet you a million pounds I do."

"I bet you a million pounds you don't," replied Darbishire.

"Take me on, then?"

"Okay."

The fate of a fortune hung in the balance as the first millionaire led his colleague towards old Pyjams.

"I say it's bananas," said Jennings. "Don't forget, you said a million, if I'm right."

They inspected the crate; it was full of bananas. "All right," said Darbishire, resigning himself to his loss with admirable fortitude. "It serves me right, I s'pose; my father says we shouldn't gamble."

Old Pyjams was wrenching the side off the crate which was marked "*Jamaican Produce*" in large stencilled letters.

"Like to bet me another million I don't know where that crate's come from?" asked Jennings, scenting further money-making possibilities.

"No, thanks. I've lost quite enough for one afternoon; I'm broke."

The ex-millionaire watched old Pyjams with interest. What was he going to do with all that wood? Perhaps he could spare a little for the model of Columbus' ship, the *Santa Maria*, that Darbishire was going to make for the end of term history modelling display. What did Jennings think?

"Prang idea!" said Jennings. "I want some wood too; I'm making a model of one of those things they used in the French Revolution that Louis XV got gelatined with."

"Don't you mean guillotined?" suggested Darbishire.

"Probably. Anyway, I've got a razor blade for the knife part," Jennings went on, "and half a bottle of red ink for the blood, but I haven't found any wood yet."

"You ask him, then," urged Darbishire.

Old Pyjams, when approached, replied that the wood was needed for his kindling. In a whispered undertone, the model-makers debated this point. Darbishire maintained that old Pyjams required the wood for his nephews and nieces.

"You know, kith and kin," he explained; "but as they're young ones they're '-ling,' like duckling, and gosling, and – er – "

"Starling?" suggested Jennings.

He approached old Pyjams again.

"I say, Robinson," he said, "d'you think your kindling wants all that wood? Would you mind asking him – er – her?"

"Them," corrected Darbishire.

"Look out!" shouted old Pyjams suddenly. Both boys jumped slightly and looked out. There, sidling furtively out between the bars of the crate, was an enormous and evil-looking spider.

"Golly," said Jennings, enchanted; "you've got a stowaway! Isn't he a beauty! He's nearly as big as my hand. I vote we capture him and – "

"Come away off on it; don't you touch 'un," warned old Pyjams. "Poison most like. Come from Jamaica it has," he went on. "Snakes and spiders, and all them foreign reptiles is poison."

He aimed a blow in its direction with a piece of wood, but the spider, with all its six eyes focused upon him, saw it coming and ran as fast as its eight legs could carry it. It took refuge beneath a bunch of bananas and waited for the all-clear.

"Don't kill it, Pyjams – er – Robinson," urged Jennings. "It might be worth a lot of money; you know, a defunct species."

"I'll bash it one and be done with it," retorted Old Pyjams. "I don't like 'em. Catch the rabies most like if it bit yer."

"Yes, but what if it's rare? I vote we catch it and take it to Mr Carter; he knows all about insects; he's a – a taximeter."

"Don't be so wet, Jen," corrected Darbishire. "A taximeter only stuffs them. Benedicks's an – an entomologist. Anyway, let's catch it, and bags it be mine."

Robinson was still anxious to leap into action with his piece of wood, but the boys persuaded him that it would be an injustice if the insect were killed before Mr Carter had identified it. The next problem was how to effect the capture without being bitten – or stung, whichever it was that a spider did. Darbishire's pencil box was voted the best way. Approaching cautiously with box and ruler at the ready, Jennings was to propel the insect into the box and Darbishire would clap down the lid. In practice it was more difficult, as both boys were extremely nervous, and the spider obstinately refused to co-operate.

"Ready?" said Jennings at the third attempt.

"Okay," said Darbishire.

"Golly, it can't half shift!" Jennings said, as the result of the manoeuvre was to send the spider scuttling in the opposite direction; but at last it was cornered and, with a twitch of the ruler, Jennings jerked it into the box and Darbishire shut the lid.

Old Pyjams was sceptical.

"Ah, eat its way through the box and all most like. I knew a chap got bit once; arm swole right up; 'ad to cut 'is sleeve to get 'is jacket orf of 'im."

"What, just from a spider's bite?"

"No; snake this was. But they're all the same, them foreign reptiles; deadly, that's what."

Clasping the box gingerly, they made their way to Mr Carter's room, but repeated knocks on the door produced no answer. The identification would have to be postponed. The dormitory was out of bounds in the daytime, but no one was about, so they decided to go there. Cautiously, they moved along the passage and opened the door; the coast was clear. The next stage of the operation was to transfer the spider from the cramped quarters of the pencil box to the more spacious surroundings of a tooth glass. This, they decided, would make an admirable observation turret where the spider could be examined more closely. It should also have the effect of putting it in a sunnier temper, when it realised how its comfort was being studied. A slight difference of opinion arose on the question of whose tooth glass should be used. Darbishire argued that Jennings' glass was the obvious choice, because Jennings had been the first to see the spider. Jennings, for the opposition, contended that the spider was the legal property of Darbishire as he had *bagsed* it, and it was the first duty of animal lovers to provide fodder and shelter for their own dumb chums. But as Darbishire was afraid that the spider's footprints might leave poisonous traces in his tooth glass, they compromised and used Temple's glass instead. This was not because they wished any harm to befall him, but because his tumbler contained smears of toothpaste which, the tube advertised, was guaranteed to kill germs, and might therefore be relied upon to remove traces of poison.

With infinite caution, Jennings opened the lid of the pencil box half an inch and peered in. The spider was sitting moodily in the middle of the box with its legs tucked in, and the dejected droop of its body seemed to suggest that it was not happy.

"He's got a sort of worried look, hasn't he?" Darbishire whispered softly, as though afraid that his normal voice would be too much for the insect to bear in its present state of woe.

"He's suffocating, that's why," Jennings explained, "or maybe he's got cramp." Quickly he opened the lid wide and clamped the inverted glass over the captive. Then he turned the glass the right way up so that the pencil box stopped doing duty as a floor and became a ceiling. The spider righted itself and stood up. With its legs extended, it stretched the width of the tumbler, and its attitude was fierce and hostile. It stood on seven legs and waved the eighth in a manner that boded evil.

"Golly, isn't he a beauty!" gasped Jennings, wonderingly. "Massive hairy legs. I say, he's in a super bate; look, he's gnashing his fangs. He looks hefty poisonous, doesn't he? Oughtn't we to get him something to eat?"

"Bananas?" suggested Darbishire.

"No, you goof. They don't live on bananas, they only live in them. Where can we get some insects from?"

"There's a fly-paper hanging up in the tuck shop," suggested Darbishire. "P'raps we could scrape some off. Bags you do it, though."

"He looks lethal poisonous now," said Jennings, as the spider stopped waving its legs and started on a tour of exploration. It made one or two attempts to walk up the side of the glass, but its efforts would hardly have inspired Robert Bruce with the determination to go out and win battles, for very soon it gave up.

"I wonder if he's a – a something like ta-ran-ta-ra?" said Jennings.

"Tarantelle," corrected Darbishire. "No, that's a dance, but it's something like that. It's bang-on dangerous if it is. I read a story once about some man-eating spiders; you don't think it's one of those, do you?" He was breathless with horrified hope.

"Might be," returned Jennings. "He seems to be drawing the line at Bod's toothpaste, though."

"I knew a joke, too, it was putridly funny." Darbishire giggled with nervous excitement. "There's some chaps talking, and somebody says to somebody else, 'Have you heard of the man-eating spiders?' And then somebody else says to another chap, or it could be the first chap; you know, the one that somebody had said to him about the man-eating spiders. Anyway, it doesn't matter which one it is, but the other chap says, 'No, but I've heard of the man-eating sandwiches.' " Darbishire became convulsed with mirth, but Jennings looked at him stonily.

"Good, isn't it?" gurgled Darbishire. "Have you heard it before?"

"No, what is it?"

"I've just told you. Somebody says to somebody else – "

"Oh, that – what's funny in that?" Jennings said, in a tone which would have spread a wet blanket over the funniest of stories. "There's no such thing as a man-eating sandwich. Anyone knows that."

"Oh, you're crackers," Darbishire objected. "You can't even see a joke."

"Oh, was it a joke? Very funny, I'm sure," he said in a dull, flat voice. "Loud titters and hearty grins!"

"Oh, shut up!" said Darbishire. "I shan't tell you any more."

The spider seemed safe enough with the pencil box acting as a roof, so they slipped a piece of chocolate into the glass in case the prisoner should feel hungry. Then they went downstairs to the library to consult the encyclopaedia. The work of identification was not easy, for there were four closely printed pages describing the anatomy and habits of dozens of spiders – several of which fitted the Jamaican stowaway perfectly. Darbishire maintained that it was either a poisonous tarantula or a bird-eating spider from South America. When Jennings pointed out that the banana crate had come from the West Indies, Darbishire contended that, as the spider was known to have made one ocean journey, it could easily have made two. His friend poured scorn on this idea of a hitch-hiking globetrotter.

"I bet it's not," he said. "I don't s'pose it's even a – a tarradiddle."

"Tarantula," Darbishire corrected, after a furtive glance at the book.

"Well, I bet it isn't. I bet you a million pounds it isn't."

"Well, I bet you two million pounds it is. Take me on?"

"You haven't got two million pounds," Jennings scoffed.

"Well, I bet you a penny then," replied Darbishire, prudently descending to brass tacks. "It's either that or a bird-eater, and if it's not that, it's so rare it's defunct, and I vote we write to the British Museum and say we've got a thing that's so defunct it isn't in the encyclopaedia, and will they please send an expert down at once to say what it is."

He paused for breath.

"Yes, rather," said Jennings. "Prang idea!"

They stood silent for a moment, for in the minds of both the boys there formed a mental picture of the arrival of the expert. Darbishire's expert was a short-sighted professor, with a long white beard and an old-fashioned frock coat, who peered intently at the spider through a magnifying glass, while making exclamations of wonder and delight. Jennings' gentleman was a tall thin man with aquiline features. He wore a uniform with brass buttons and, above the shiny black peak of his regulation cap, the words "British Museum" were inscribed in letters of silver wire.

"I vote we don't tell Benedick till the Museum's been, or he'll want a share of the reward," Darbishire said.

"What reward?"

Darbishire insisted that some recognition of their services was almost inevitable, for if the spider was rare, the cream of the insect-studying world would hurry from all parts to write books about it; on the other hand, if it was a crop-destroying pest, a grateful government would not be slow to reward public benefactors. Jennings was sceptical; it seemed unlikely to him that the captive was anything but a large and hairy-legged insect with no instinct to harm anyone, and he was all in favour of consulting Mr Carter before calling in the British Museum. Still, it was Darbishire's spider, so he did not pursue the matter.

The bell rang for afternoon preparation before Darbishire's letter was begun, and he went into the classroom bursting to tell everyone the news. After preparation and during football practice the news spread with lightning rapidity, and the school buzzed with excitement and shuddered with horror as they heard that Darbishire's death-dealing monster was imprisoned in the dormitory.

"I say, have you heard the latest? Darbi's got a hefty smash-on spider. It's as hairy as a ruin and super lethal."

"Stale buns! I knew that a hundred years ago; Jennings told me, and he said Darbishire was trying to make out that it eats sandwiches."

"No, it doesn't then, 'cos he looked it up in the encyclopaedia; it's something Latin; tarantula or something."

"I bet that's not Latin."

"Course it is. It goes like *mensa*. Tarantula – tarantula – tarantulam – tarantula – tarantulae – tarantula. So that proves it."

"Shut up, we've got Latin this afternoon; we don't want any more now."

The group in the classroom ceased their speculation as Darbishire entered, wearing a dignified look suitable to one who has heavy entomologic responsibilities.

"Hallo, you chaps," announced the entomologist. "Anyone like to do me a favour? It's spivish important."

"I will," said Atkinson.

"Well, I've been doing some research, and my latest theory is that my spider's definitely a bird-eating one, so will you go and find old Pyjams and tell him to be sure not to let the hens out till the British Museum's been." There were still five minutes before afternoon school at four o'clock, and Atkinson sped on his errand of mercy while Darbishire continued his scientific discourse.

"Old Pyjams said that if it bites you, your arm swells up and they have to cut your coat sleeve to get it off – your coat, I mean, not your arm. He just took one look at the spider and he knew. It happened to a friend of his, you see, so we know it must be true."

The younger members of the group felt a little uneasy, but Darbishire, with his expert knowledge, was able to assure them that the spider was quite safe in its observation turret, and they need have nothing to fear.

The necessity of writing at once to the British Museum was uppermost in his mind during afternoon school, and several times he was in trouble for not attending to the lesson, but the bell rang at last and, surrounded by an awe-struck throng, he produced his writing-pad.

"I think I'll write direct to the manager," he said, "and tell him I've got a gargantuan tarantula – if I can spell it."

"I thought you said it came from Jamaica?" queried Venables.

"So it does; gargantuan means the size, not the place. The Museum'll be wizard interested, I should think; they might even make me a Fellow."

"Jolly good!"

"No, just an ordinary one," said Darbishire. "I'm a bit worried about what to feed him on, though. We tried him with chocolate, but I think he was off his food a bit, 'cos he wouldn't look at it."

"Coo, super daring!" breathed Atkinson admiringly. "I wouldn't like to feed him. Ugh!" He shuddered, and ran spidery fingers down the neck of the boy standing beside him.

"Oh, it's quite easy," Darbishire said modestly. "Of course you've got to know something about taxid – er – ornith – er – it's easy if you know anything about insects. Jennings hypnotised him, while I popped the chocolate in."

The group pressed him for details of how to put spiders under hypnotic spells.

"Well," he said, "you have to fix it with a glittering eye, like the old codger in the poem who shot an albatross – Paul Revere or whatever his name was. You just do to the spider what he did to the wedding guests, and it stands still and doesn't move."

It was always shepherd's pie for tea on Fridays, and Jennings made as poor a meal as he had done the previous week. The injustice of fate spoiled his appetite and made him miserable. Last week he had been unable to play in the match because he was ill, and now that he was fit, Mr Wilkins had spoiled everything. He knew that he himself was partly to blame, and he knew, because everyone made it abundantly clear, that his guilt would long be remembered in the minds of his fellows. He decided to go and see Mr Wilkins, and plead with him to alter his decision. He would say he was willing to take the punishment, if only the others might be allowed to play the match, as arranged.

After evening preparation he went to Mr Wilkins' room, but there was no reply to his knock, so he decided to call back later and to pass the time in watching Darbishire's spider. No one was about, so he slipped into the dormitory. There it was, still standing in its observation turret. Like Jennings, it had lost its appetite, and had made no attempt to eat its piece of chocolate. He gazed at it long and earnestly. It was certainly a beautiful specimen, but Jennings could not share Darbishire's belief that it was either so poisonous or so rare that the work of the British Museum must be interrupted. How stupid they would look if it turned out to be harmless after all! In his imagination, he could see innumerable experts chafing and complaining at the way their time had been wasted, while the Headmaster stood by ready to take action when the experts had departed. Surely Mr Carter would know; he was an expert of sorts, even though he didn't wear a uniform with brass buttons.

Jennings picked up his soap dish from the washbasin, washed it out, and turned his attention once more to the spider. He removed the pencil box from the tumbler and replaced it with the soap dish. A quick movement and the spider somersaulted from the upturned glass into the dish, and the top was placed firmly into position. Carefully, Jennings left the tooth glass and pencil box as he had found them, and departed to Mr Carter's room.

Mr Carter looked up from his desk.

"Come in, Jennings," he said. "What can I do for you?"

"Please, sir, do you know anything about taximeters?"

"No, practically nothing," Mr Carter replied. "Why?"

"But I thought insects were your hobby, sir?"

Mr Carter explained the difference between a taxidermist, who stuffs animals, and an entomologist, who studies insects, and Jennings gingerly removed the cover from his soap dish.

"My word, he's a fine fellow," said Mr Carter. "Where did you come across him?"

"In Temple's tooth glass, sir."

"Uh!" Mr Carter looked puzzled. It seemed an odd place for such a discovery.

"And before that he was in a crate of bananas, sir," Jennings explained. "Robinson says your arm swells up if it bites you, and Darbishire's going to get the British Museum to call, but I didn't think it was a tarran something, so I borrowed it to ask you, sir."

Mr Carter looked at the spider and then, to Jennings' horror, he picked it up and held it in the palm of his hand.

"Sorry to disappoint Darbishire," he said; "but this chap's quite harmless."

"Isn't he even poisonous of any kind?"

"Not even of any kind." He turned his hand over as the spider, savouring its newly-found liberty, stretched its legs and ran on to the back of Mr Carter's hand and made for his sleeve. "No, you can't go up there," said Mr Carter, gently removing the insect. He put it on his blotting-pad where, after running a few steps, it stood still as though deep in thought.

"I'm afraid he looks rather startling," Mr Carter said, as though apologising for the spider's appearance, "but he's quite gentle, really. He wouldn't hurt a fly! Or rather, he would hurt a fly, but he wouldn't hurt anything else," he amended.

As there seemed no prospect of Mr Carter's coat sleeve having to be cut off, Jennings took courage and picked the insect from the blotter and replaced it in the soap dish. The dormitory bell sounded, and Jennings prepared to leave.

"I'd better put it back in the tooth glass, then, sir," he said, " 'cos Darbishire doesn't know I've got it, and he'll be rather worried if he thinks it's escaped." The telephone rang as Jennings was making for the door, and Mr Carter picked up the receiver.

"Hallo, Linbury Court here... Who?... Bracebridge School?... Oh, yes."

Jennings started guiltily at the mention of Bracebridge, and the soap dish slipped from his hand and fell open on the carpet. The spider made a dash for liberty and took cover behind a bookcase. Quickly, Jennings cut off its retreat by blocking the bookcase at one end, and then set about the difficult task of poking behind the books with a pencil, in order to drive the spider back into the open.

It was not that he meant to listen to Mr Carter's conversation on the telephone, but he could not go while the spider was still at large, and he found it impossible to help overhearing what Mr Carter was saying.

"What's that? You're coming over tomorrow after, all?" Mr Carter said into the telephone. "But Mr Parkinson rang me up at break this morning and cancelled it; he said you'd had German measles."

Jennings pricked up his ears and completely forgot the spider as he focused his mind on this unexpected development. He waited, hardly daring to breathe, while Mr Carter listened to what was obviously a long and involved explanation from the other end of the line.

Then Mr Carter said, "Oh, I see. Yes, I believe you're right. It is only three weeks for German measles, and if you started on the fourteenth, you'd be out of quarantine yesterday."

The unseen voice buzzed again.

"Yes," said Mr Carter. "When Parkinson said a month, I took his word for it. Well, I'm very glad anyway, and we'll expect you tomorrow at two-thirty as we arranged... Right. Goodbye." He replaced the receiver and turned to see Jennings kneeling by the bookcase.

"What are you doing here, Jennings?" he asked. "I thought you had gone."

Jennings explained how the spider's bid for freedom had delayed him, and Mr Carter got down on his knees and together they tried to entice the insect from its retreat. And all the time Jennings was thinking furiously. If Bracebridge had cancelled the match because of its German measles, the uproar in the classroom couldn't have been the genuine reason. Furthermore, if Bracebridge had 'phoned during morning break, Mr Wilkins must have known that the game was cancelled before he imposed the punishment. And now there was some further complication, and they were coming after all. It was all very confusing.

"Well, you haven't helped much," said Mr Carter. He rose to his feet and placed the spider back in the soap dish. "You'd better tell Darbishire to let it go; outside somewhere, not in the building."

"Sir," said Jennings. "Mr Wilkins said the match was scratched because I didn't turn the tap on, and everyone made a row; and you said on the 'phone – "

"That 'phone call, Jennings, was a private conversation between Bracebridge School and me."

"Yes, but Mr Wilkins can't do that, can he, sir? It's not fair; and what'll happen tomorrow when they turn up?"

Mr Carter said, "Go to bed, Jennings, and don't ask so many questions. You remember what happened to the Elephant's Child with his 'satiable curtiosity?"

"Yes, sir," said Jennings. When he got to the door he paused. "Yes, but, sir – "

"It's entirely a matter between you and Mr Wilkins," Mr Carter informed him. "And if he says that your form has to be in detention tomorrow afternoon, that's that, as far as I'm concerned."

"Yes, sir," said Jennings. "I wasn't going to argue, sir; I was only going to say that the Elephant's Child may have been nosey, but he did pretty well for himself in the end, didn't he, sir?"

On the landing outside, Jennings met Mr Wilkins and delivered his carefully thought out speech.

"Sir," he began, "I must see you, sir. It's urgent."

Mr Wilkins was not pleased to see him.

"Well?" he said.

"Sir, will you keep me in tomorrow and not the others? Honestly, sir, it wasn't their fault, and they're down on me like anything."

I'm not surprised," said Mr Wilkins, not without satisfaction. "And what's more, I'm not altering my punishment. When I say something, it goes." He'd let them see he was someone to be reckoned with.

Jennings was about to explain that there was some mystery about the cancellation of the match, but Mr Wilkins cut him short.

"You're late for dormitory, and you haven't changed into your house shoes. Go downstairs and do it at once."

Still clasping the soap dish, with the spider inside, Jennings descended to the basement, while Mr Wilkins went to call upon Mr Carter. He found him filling his pipe and wearing an amused smile which he was doing his best to conceal.

"Oh, Wilkins," he said. "Bracebridge have just been through on the 'phone. Apparently Parkinson thought that the quarantine period for German measles was one month."

"Well?" demanded Mr Wilkins, suspiciously.

"It isn't; it's only twenty-one days; and as they've not had any more cases in the last three weeks, we can play them tomorrow without fear of catching anything."

Mr Wilkins appeared stunned by the news.

"What?" he gasped.

This new development would make a hollow mockery of his drastic punishment. True, he could keep Form Three in detention during the match, if he insisted, but he grew hot and cold when he thought of the triumphant smiles that would greet the news when it was announced.

It was a delicate situation, in all conscience, and if he insisted on his detention now that the match was going to be played, his action would merely weaken the First Eleven, and it would be his fault if the school lost the game.

"What am I going to do?" he asked. "When I cancelled the

game this morning, they got a nasty jolt they hadn't bargained for. They'll laugh their heads off if I climb down now."

"Well, I did warn you," Mr Carter said. "I think you'll have to find a reason to let them off."

"Yes," said Mr Wilkins. "But how? Needs thinking out, doesn't it?"

His blustering manner had departed; he left Mr Carter's study deep in thought, and wandered off to take duty in the dormitories.

11

Beware of the Thing!

At the first sound of the dormitory bell, Darbishire led the way upstairs, with the excited spectators at his heels. Only Dormitory Four would be privileged to see the spider in all its glory, for the boys were not allowed into any room except their own. But in order to alleviate the disappointment of the rest of the school, Darbishire had agreed to take the observation turret for a short walk along the corridor, so that the eager throng might enjoy a brief glimpse of the pride of the species *Araneae*. With Temple, Venables and Atkinson pressing close behind, he flung wide the dormitory door and made a bee-line for the tumbler on the shelf.

"We must be careful not to frighten it," he said, " 'cos it's probably super sensitive and – "

He stopped dead some three feet from the shelf. The expression of self-satisfied importance slid from his features like a landslide, and was replaced by a look of amazed horror. He stared wide-eyed and open-mouthed at the empty tumbler. "Oh, golly!" he gasped. "Oh, gosh! It's – it's escaped!"

"What!" Aghast, the spectators pressed nearer and, as the evidence of the empty glass confirmed the tidings, they stepped gingerly away out of range.

"It must have crawled up the glass and squeezed its way

171

out," Darbishire continued excitedly. "Yes, look, the pencil box has been moved; it's got edged over a bit since Jen and I left it. Oh, golly, what are we going to do? It's lethal dangerous, don't forget."

The little group stood awkwardly, nervously silent. A cautious survey of the shelf revealed no trace of the spider and, with some misgivings, they decided that a thorough search was the only solution to the difficulty.

"It must be somewhere in the dorm," said Temple, glancing nervously over his shoulder. "We're bound to find it if we look. Mind out if anyone sees it, though. We mustn't touch it because of its deadly venom."

"Supposing it rushes at us?" Atkinson inquired timidly. "What'll we do?"

Darbishire replied, without conviction. "We'll have to try hypnotising it. Pity Jennings is late coming up; he's rare at doing that."

Treading with the utmost delicacy, they started the hunt; all except Atkinson, who was scared to move from the centre of the floor for fear he should accidentally tread on the object of their search. The thought that the spider might be ensconced in someone's bed, or nestling snugly in the folds of someone's pyjamas, did nothing to lessen their uneasiness, and in the intervals of their cautious peering, Darbishire's entomological exploits came in for some harsh criticism.

"You are a dangerous maniac, Darbi," Temple said. "Just because you want to be made a jolly good fellow of the British Museum, we have to suffer, and now we can't even get into bed."

"Well, how was I to know it could get out?" Darbishire defended himself. "Must have got hairy strength."

"Anyone knows a great hefty spider like that could have pushed a box off the top," Temple went on. "I expect it made a great leap as soon as your back was turned, and now it's sitting in a corner laughing at us and waiting to spring."

"Oh, shut up," said Darbishire, thoroughly rattled. "Let's go on looking." With infinite caution, he lifted a piece of soap and searched beneath, and in his agitation he swept a tooth brush off a basin with his elbow. The brush fell to the floor with the faintest of clatters, but the four boys started violently and spun round in the direction of the sound.

Darbishire gulped and said, "All right, chaps; false alarm. We must go on looking, but for goodness' sake don't let it bite you!"

"No fear," added Venables, " 'cos your arm swells up like a balloon, don't forget, and they have to cut your jacket off."

"I vote we all take our jackets off first, then," suggested Atkinson.

"Fat lot of good that'd be if it bit you in the foot," Temple retorted. "It'd be more sense to put our gum boots on in case it nips us on the ankle."

Darbishire thought that the boys in the other dormitories should be warned, in case the spider had gone on a voyage of exploration. He was not keen to make the announcement personally, as experience in his own dormitory had taught him that the news would not be sympathetically received. He decided, therefore, to compromise and display a warning notice on the door, so that passers-by in the corridor might be put on their guard. He had a small piece of white chalk in his pocket, so he tiptoed into the corridor and paused to consider the wording of his notice. He would like to have written, "*Beware of the dangerous gargantuan tarantula which is not now in captivity*," but he had not enough chalk for so lengthy a warning. He shortened the notice and started off, "*Beware of the –* " but without the encyclopaedia to refer to, he was uncertain how to spell tarantula, and there was also the doubt that the spider might belong to some other species, anyway.

Finally, he wrote, "*Beware of the Thing!*" in large capitals and left the rest of the school to puzzle over this cryptic warning for the remainder of the evening.

He returned to his dormitory, where the search was still going on in a timid and half-hearted fashion, for no one dared to make a thorough investigation under or behind articles of furniture which might conceal the lurking foe.

Temple said, with a sigh of relief: "Well, it's not in my pyjamas, anyway, thank goodness. Have you looked in your bedroom slippers, Venables?"

"Yes," Venables said uncertainly; "but I can't see right up to the end of them."

"Put your hand in, then, and feel," suggested Atkinson.

"Oh, yes, and get my fingers bitten. No, thanks!" Darbishire lowered himself gingerly on to his hands and knees, and peered under the beds. Suddenly, a strangled cry broke from his lips and the other boys leapt like startled deer.

"What's the matter, Darbi?"

"Did it get you, Darbi? Are you all right?"

"Shall I go and get Matron?"

The whole dormitory was alert and attentive, and Atkinson had already produced his nail scissors in order to cut the victim's coat sleeve, when Darbishire announced that his discovery was only a piece of fluff.

"It looked just like it, though," he explained.

But this fresh shock had unnerved them. The thought that the deadly enemy might be lurking in sponge bag, dressing-gown or towel, was a terrifying one.

"We might even have to get the floor boards up to find it," Temple said helplessly. "It's not safe to get undressed, let alone get into bed."

"And if we did get into bed," added Atkinson, "it might suddenly rush at us in the dark and we'd all wake up like swollen balloons... Swollen balloons!" he repeated in awe-struck tones, as a covey of elephantine barrage balloons drifted across his imagination. He shuddered, and then rose quickly from the bed on which he had thoughtlessly seated himself.

Something had to be done, and as none of them felt safe standing by their beds within reach of the spider's fangs, Darbishire suggested that they should put their bedside chairs in the middle of the room and stand on them. This would keep their feet clear of the floor and enable them to see the approach of the foe. Walking as delicately as Agag, the boys assembled their chairs and climbed up to commence their vigil.

After a strained and miserable silence which lasted for nearly a minute, Atkinson spoke the question which was uppermost in all their minds.

"Have we got to stand like this all night?" he said.

"Jolly well hope not," Venables muttered. "Gosh, you are a maniacal lunatic, Darbishire."

"I'm going to find Wilkie," announced Temple. "He's on duty, so he ought to know how to deal with venomous spiders, or if he can't, p'raps he could get the British Museum to hurry up a bit, otherwise" – he shrugged his shoulders helplessly – "otherwise we'll have to evacuate."

Temple departed on his errand, but it took him some time to locate the master on duty. This was unusual, for normally Mr Wilkins spent the bedtime half-hour in bursting into each dormitory every few minutes with injunctions to "Get a move on and take a brush to those knees." But this evening he had retired to Matron's sitting-room, where although officially on duty, he could find the peace and quiet necessary for one who had a problem to resolve.

The school clock struck eight, and down in the boot-room

Jennings suddenly realised that he had wasted ten minutes in changing his house shoes. True, he had spent most of the time in giving the spider an airing, and admiring its style as it sidled majestically round the boot-lockers, but the chimes of the clock reminded him that he would have to hurry if he was to be in bed before the bell. He picked the spider from the toe of a football boot where it had been marking time gracefully, and replaced it in the soap dish. Golly, he'd have to hurry, and Darbishire would be getting worried about what had become of his rare specimen. How small he would feel when told that his spider was quite harmless!

Clasping the soap dish, he made his way upstairs, unaware just how worried Darbishire actually was.

At the door, he paused to read the notice: "*Beware of the Thing!*" What on earth did that mean? They must be crazy! When he opened the door and saw Darbishire, Atkinson and Venables standing forlornly on their chairs as though in fear of some rising tide, he was quite sure of it. They certainly were crazy!

"What are you all doing up there?" he asked.

"It's the spider," Darbishire replied in a nervous voice. "It's got loose. Get your chair and bring it over here if you want to be safe."

"Yes, don't stand there like that," urged Atkinson. "It might charge at you suddenly and then you'd be liquidated."

A slow smile spread across Jennings' features as he realised what had happened.

"Well, you are a lot of funks," he said scornfully, as he placed the soap dish on the shelf above his bed. "Fancy being scared of a little tin-pot spider!" And he laughed contemptuously as he took off his jacket and shoes.

"You – you're not going to get into bed, are you?" gasped Venables.

"Of course I am; I'm not scared." Jennings hummed gaily to prove it.

"Coo, super daring," breathed Atkinson. "I wouldn't. You know what'll happen if it nips you, don't you? Balloons!" And with one finger he sketched the uncomfortable outline in the air above his head.

Jennings dismissed the danger with a laugh and, proceeded to get undressed. He was aware of the sensation he was causing, and his movements were casual and slow as befitted one who cares nought for danger. He sang snatches of song in the intervals of telling the others how cowardly they were. They were awe-struck and envious, but they did not dare to follow his example. Jennings was enjoying every minute of it. From time to time he stole a glance at the soap dish, but all was well; it gave no sign of its guilty secret.

Presently Darbishire said: "Mind how you turn your bed down, Jennings." And a second later he yelled aloud: "Look out!"

Even Jennings jumped, although he knew there was no danger, while Atkinson and Venables nearly fell off their chairs in their agitation.

With a dramatic sweep of the hand, Darbishire pointed to Jennings' pillow.

"There," he croaked. "Look! The poisonous spider's venomous footprints."

Jennings inspected his pillow.

"Oh, rats!" he replied. "Those are cake crumbs. I foxed a hunk up to eat in bed last night, but it went all crumbly and got all over the sheet. Massive tickly." A mischievous expression came into his eyes. "Not so tickly as the fangs of a dangerous spider, though," he went on, his voice shaking in mock horror. Then he burst out laughing. "You do look funny up there," he gurgled. "You are a lot of funks! Who's frightened of a titchy little incey-wincey spider?

"Incey-wincey spider, climbed the waterspout,
 Down came the rain and washed the spider
    out,"

he recited gleefully.

"You're just a swank," said Venables, but he was unable to conceal a trace of admiration in his voice.

"Jennings may be very brave," commented Darbishire; "but he's behaving most recklessly. My father says that discretion is the better part of valour, so I'm staying up here till Wilkie comes to tell us what to do."

"Oh, goodness!" said Jennings, his wave of enjoyment ebbing visibly. "Does Wilkie know about this?"

"Bod's gone to fetch him," said Atkinson.

Jennings thought for a moment. He had decided to make a last appeal to Mr Wilkins to reconsider his decision to punish the form, and it would not improve matters if Mr Wilkins thought that Jennings was responsible for this new interference with the smooth-running of the school routine.

"I say, Darbi," he said. "Come outside on the landing a mo'; I want to talk to you privately."

"I daren't get down," said Darbishire, unhappily.

"But it's urgent. Look, you can see it's clear as far as the door. I'll convoy you and hypnotise the spider if it jumps out of an ambush and attacks us."

With some misgiving, Darbishire left his perch and followed Jennings on to the landing.

"Well?" he demanded.

"Look, it's quite all right about the spider," Jennings assured him in a conspiratorial whisper. "It's in the soap dish on the shelf over my bed. I borrowed it to show Benedick, and he says it's quite harmless, unless you're a fly."

"Honest injun?"

"Yes."

"Coo! What a swizzle!"

Relief at their safe deliverance was mingled with disappointment that the spider was not a rare specimen after all. "Good job I haven't posted my letter to the Museum yet," Darbishire said, and then another aspect struck him which was almost as unpleasant to think about as the ordeal through which they had just passed.

"Golly!" he said. "What'll the other chaps say when they find out? They'll think I've been fooling them; they'll never believe me after all this hoo-hah if I just walk in with a light laugh and say it isn't poisonous after all. They're bound to say I knew all the time and then I'll get bashed up for pulling their legs."

"You'd better keep quiet about it, then," Jennings advised.

"Yes, but I can't let them go on thinking it's dangerous and leave them standing on chairs all night. Oh, gosh, I wish I'd never found the beastly thing, and I was counting on that reward from the British Museum to buy a meccano set with, too."

Jennings pointed out that this was not the only difficulty. If they were to produce the spider forthwith and announce it to be harmless, Mr Wilkins would think that Jennings had borrowed it specially to spread alarm and despondency throughout the dormitory. And though this was not the case, Mr Wilkins would be only too ready to believe the worst and would be in no mood to cancel the detention.

"Wilkie'll get into a hefty bate if he knows I had anything to do with it," he went on. "You see, there's just a chance there may be a match tomorrow after all, so I've got to get him in a good mood."

"What had we better do, then?" Darbishire wanted to know.

179

"Well, the less either of us has to do with finding the wretched thing, the better. You, 'cos you'll get bashed up, and me, 'cos Wilkie'll think I pinched it to put the wind up everyone."

They decided that the best thing to do was to remove the lid of the soap dish without being seen, and allow someone else to make the discovery. The spider could then be caught and disposed of without anyone suspecting its non-poisonous qualities. They returned to the dormitory again and Darbishire mounted his chair to allay suspicion. A moment later he shouted "Look!" and pointed to the far end of the room. Atkinson and Venables turned horrified eyes in the required direction, and while their attention was diverted, Jennings reached up and took the lid off the soap dish.

"Oh, sorry," said Darbishire, "another false alarm; it must have been that splodge on the wall I was looking at."

Atkinson and Venables turned shakily away from the false alarm, and their eyes continued to rove round the room in their ceaseless quest. But, although their gaze passed frequently over the shelf above Jennings' bed, neither of them noticed the spider. It was so obviously visible that Jennings and Darbishire had difficulty in keeping their eyes away from it, and the spider seemed to be doing its best to attract attention by making little darting, sallies along the shelf.

Jennings became anxious at the delay; he wanted the spider safely imprisoned before Mr Wilkins arrived, so that his innocence would be unquestioned, and he would be free to open up the vexed question of the detention.

Heavy footsteps on the landing outside indicated that Mr Wilkins was approaching. He had not been feeling in the best of tempers when Temple had run him to earth in Matron's sitting-room, and the news that he was required to round up a dangerous insect was not well received. Heedless of the warning on the dormitory door, Mr Wilkins strode in, followed by Temple, who appeared relieved to see that all present were still fit and well.

"Now, what's all this tom-foolery about?" Mr Wilkins barked. "What are you boys doing on those chairs? Get down at once."

"But, sir, it's poisonous," protested Venables, "we daren't get down. It isn't tom-foolery, really, sir."

The serious note in his voice made Mr Wilkins pause.

"Let's get this straight," he said. "Temple comes to me burbling like a half-wit with some cock-and-bull story about a spider. Well, how d'you know it's poisonous for a start?"

"But we proved it, sir," Temple assured him. "Darbishire looked it up in the encyclopaedia; it's either a tarantula or something like a blank window."

"What?" said Mr Wilkins, at sea.

"Black widow, sir," corrected Darbishire.

"And it came out of a crate of bananas," Temple went on. "And Robinson said it was just like one that bit a friend of his."

"And he 'swoled' up like a balloon," added Atkinson.

Mr Wilkins knew nothing of insects. It might be true or it might not, but it would be better not to take risks in a case of this kind.

"All right," he said, seizing a hairbrush; "we'll take precautions and have a thorough search."

"Shall I go and fetch you a cricket bat, sir?" asked Temple, eager to assist. "You can have mine willingly. It's locked up for the winter, but I can easily get the key and – "

"No, sir, have mine," urged Venables, "it's full size; Temple's is only a size four."

"Sir, mine's got a rubber handle on, sir," Atkinson put in. "Unfortunately I left it at home last hols, but if I'd thought, I could have brought it back and it'd be super, wouldn't it, sir?"

"Be quiet, all of you," Mr Wilkins ordered.

"I've got some batting gloves at home, too, sir," added Atkinson. "They'd be a bit small for you, even if I'd got them here, but they've got rubber fingers, and – "

"Will you stop this chattering!" Mr Wilkins sounded annoyed, and Jennings decided to broach the question of the punishment before the situation became any worse.

"Please, sir," he said. "I wanted to talk to you about the detention. I'm quite willing to stay in if you'll let the others off."

Mr Wilkins was exasperated beyond measure.

"For goodness' sake, Jennings, can't you see I've got something more important to do than talk about detention. This is a serious business. If this spider's really poisonous it – it – well, it might bite someone."

"Yes, sir, but this detention – "

"Go away. Go and stand on a chair with the others."

Jennings gave it' up for the time being; he took his chair and joined the group in the middle of the room.

Mr Wilkins glared round the dormitory defiantly; he brandished the hairbrush as though challenging the spider to come out and fight.

"Well, I can't see any sign of it," he said. He moved towards Jennings' bed and prodded a dressing-gown with the hairbrush. By now he was standing immediately below the shelf, while the spider performed a ceremonial war-dance just above his head.

Jennings and Darbishire watched entranced, and it was with the greatest difficulty that they held their peace. From their vantage point on the chairs, it was clearly visible. If only the others would stop looking at Mr Wilkins and raise their eyes to the shelf above. Then Temple saw it…!

"Oooh!" he gasped.

Mr Wilkins turned.

"What's the matter, boy?"

"I can see it, sir."

"You can? Where? Let me get at it."

"No, sir, don't move, sir," Temple warned him. "Don't even bat an eyelid, sir."

"But where is it, you silly little boy?" demanded Mr Wilkins, looking in every direction except the right one.

They had all seen it now.

"Keep still, sir, don't move," called Atkinson. He gripped his nail scissors firmly, ready to deal with any sleeve-cutting crisis that might arise.

"I'll throw a slipper at it," Venables suggested.

"No, don't do that," Jennings reproved him. "You might miss and hit Mr Wilkins. Sir, about this detention, sir..." he began again.

Mr Wilkins was rattled; he knew the foe was close at hand, and this was no time to talk about detention.

"I can't see the beastly thing," he said. "Where is it?"

"It's about an inch above your head," answered Temple shrilly. "It's coming nearer – it's on the edge now; it's taking off – oh, sir, keep still; it's touched down on your shoulder."

Mr Wilkins aimed a sharp blow at his left shoulder, and out of the corner of his eye, he caught his first glimpse of the spider. It was on his right shoulder and walking determinedly towards his collar. Mr Wilkins froze; rigid and motionless he stood, and the spider did the same. Mr Wilkins made a movement with his left hand and immediately the spider resumed his walk. Mr Wilkins stopped, and the spider stopped. It was clear to Mr Wilkins that if he made any further movement, the spider would continue along its dangerous course. The only way to postpone an encounter at unpleasantly close quarters, was to remain perfectly still.

Unfortunately, the insect was so close to his collar by this time, that he could not see it without twisting his head, and every movement made an attack more imminent. For five seconds both Mr Wilkins and the spider might have been statues; then the larger of the two opponents spoke out of the corner of his mouth.

"What's it doing now?" he asked.

"It's giving you a sort of look, sir," Temple said.

"Stand still, you boys," Mr Wilkins ordered; "I'm going to knock it off with a sharp blow."

"It might bite your hand, sir," objected Atkinson.

For half a second Mr Wilkins considered.

"Here, Darbishire," he said, "you looked this thing up in the book; which end bites – the back or the front?"

"All over, I think, sir," replied Darbishire. "And, anyway, I don't know one end from the other."

A strangled gasp from Temple indicated that the spider had become tired of this waiting game and was about to make a practice run over the target area. The situation was desperate, and Mr Wilkins did not like it at all.

Suddenly Jennings stepped down from his chair and approached the master with hand outstretched.

"It's all right, sir," he said. "Keep still and I'll get it off."

"Don't touch it boy; don't touch it," warned Mr Wilkins.

"But I know how to handle it, sir. I can hypnotise it, sir, honestly." Jennings stared hard and the spider returned his gaze. Then he gently picked the insect from Mr Wilkins' collar and placed it safely in a tooth glass.

For some seconds the spectators were dumbfounded; then slowly they recovered the power of speech.

"Coo!" they murmured reverently. "Coo!... Gosh!... You have got a nerve, Jennings."

Jennings smiled modestly.

The tension was eased now that the danger had passed;

everyone breathed sighs of relief and, slightly disappointed, Atkinson put his nail scissors back in their case.

"Jolly daring, wasn't it, sir?" said Temple. "Why, p'raps Jennings has even saved your life, sir."

"Well done, Jennings! Super prang nerve!" The dormitory was unanimous in its praise.

"Er – yes, thank you very much, Jennings, I'm grateful," said Mr Wilkins. "Of course, I could have coped with it quite easily, myself, in the normal way, but it had me – er – it had me at a disadvantage. Very plucky of you; it does you credit."

"That's all right, sir," Jennings replied. "I didn't want you to suffer, sir. And sir – sir, about this detention; it was all my fault, really, and I was wondering whether – that is – "

He stopped, as though reluctant to ask a favour of one who was so much in his debt that he could hardly refuse. Here was the answer to Mr Wilkins' dilemma; it was his cue and he took it.

"Ah, yes, the detention," he said. "Well, now, we've just witnessed a – er – an extremely commendable action on Jennings' part."

"Hear, hear," said Darbishire.

"So in recognition of the – er – "

"Meritorious conduct," prompted Darbishire.

"Be quiet, Darbishire. In recognition of this – er – of this, I shall cancel the detention for tomorrow afternoon."

"Coo, thank you, sir!" The dormitory waved their sponge bags round their heads in appreciation.

"And I'll go further," Mr Wilkins added generously, "the match against Bracebridge will take place, as arranged. The cancellation is – er – cancelled."

"Hooray! Super-wizzo-duper! Smash-on!" Dormitory Four cheered the good news to the echo, while Mr Wilkins stood smiling and satisfied.

"And now if you'll hand me that tooth glass, Jennings," he said, "I'll take the beastly thing downstairs and kill it."

"Oh, no, please don't, do that, sir," Darbishire pleaded.

"But it's dangerous!"

"Oh, but, sir, it's only – "

Jennings trod on Darbishire's toes warningly.

"...Ow! Shut up, Jennings. I – I mean it's only poisonous if you don't know how to handle it."

Mr Wilkins refused to allow the insect to remain a danger to all and sundry, so Jennings suggested that Mr Carter should be asked to despatch it humanely in his butterfly killing bottle.

"Then he can give it back to us and we can stuff it," he suggested.

"Stuff it?" repeated Mr Wilkins, surprised.

"Yes, sir," Jennings answered. "Like a taxi – er – a taxi – what d'you call it?"

"Entomologist," corrected Darbishire.

"That's right. I know where we can get some straw to stuff it with," he went on excitedly.

"Straw wouldn't do for this," said Darbishire. "It'd need sawdust or feathers, and p'r'aps we ought to get some buttons for the eyes, like they have for stags and things."

"H'm," said Mr Wilkins. "It's going to look an odd sort of specimen by the time you've finished with it. Hurry up and get into bed; this light should have been out ten minutes ago."

He left them making arrangements to exhibit the spider in the school museum.

"We could make a glass case," Jennings was saying, "and have an inscription engraved – it'd have to be in Latin, though, if it's a tarantula, 'cos it goes like *mensa*, and that's first declension."

Mr Carter looked up from his desk as Mr Wilkins entered

with a tumbler containing a familiar occupant.

"I say, Carter," he said, "will you put this ghastly insect in your killing bottle. The wretched thing nearly bit me just now; if it hadn't been for some pretty prompt action by Jennings, I might be in a rather bad state by this time."

Mr Carter smiled and reached for the tooth glass.

"It's no laughing matter," said Mr Wilkins. "It's poisonous. Here, don't touch it," he shouted, as Mr Carter tipped the spider into the palm of his hand.

"Oh, no, it's not," Mr Carter assured him. "It's quite harmless. I told Jennings it was when he brought it in earlier this evening."

Mr Wilkins' jaw dropped slightly at this new revelation.

"What?" he gasped. "You told – ? You mean Jennings knew that the thing was harmless all the time? And he let me… Cor-wumph!" he exploded. "So that was the game, was it?"

Mr Carter didn't follow.

"But, dash it, he – he picked it off my collar and I congratulated him on his bravery!"

"Did Jennings tell you it was poisonous?"

"Well, no, he didn't," Mr Wilkins admitted; "but everybody else seemed to think it was, and I said they could play the match tomorrow because of his conduct."

Mr Carter pointed out that Mr Wilkins would have had to have done that, anyway. "It gave you a very good excuse," he said.

"Yes, I know, but…" Mr Wilkins sawed the air in his effort to find the right words to describe his feelings. "…Dash it, Carter, the wretched little boy must have been… Right! I'll see he doesn't get away with it… It's – cor-wumph – it's – dash it, it's deceitful."

Mr Carter filled his pipe while the storm blew itself out. Then he said:

"I don't think I'd take the matter any further, Wilkins; you see, Jennings, was here when the 'phone message came through from Bracebridge, and quite by accident he found out that your scratching the match this morning was – well, not cricket."

"Oh!" Mr Wilkins stopped fuming, and became quietly thoughtful.

"So all things considered," Mr Carter went on, "I think it'd be better to let sleeping dogs lie, don't you?"

Mr Wilkins stood silently for a moment, tracing a pattern on the carpet with the toe of his shoe. At last he spoke.

"H'm… Yes, perhaps you're right, Carter," he said slowly. "…Perhaps you're right."

12

Jennings Uses His Head

Jennings spent most of Saturday morning with his fingers crossed. So many obstacles had arisen to block his path to the First Eleven, that he could hardly believe that they had been successfully overcome. Now, however, with bilious attacks and, detentions safely behind him, there was nothing to stop him from realising his ambition. All the same, he was on his guard lest fate should intervene with another cruel blow.

His usual method of going down to breakfast was to take the stairs two at a time, and the last three in one enormous leap, but today he walked sedately, grasping the banisters firmly in case a chance slip should result in a sprained ankle. Carefully he scanned the faces at the breakfast table, fearful lest some wretched creature had come out in spots during the night and it would be Linbury's turn to telephone messages of cancellation. However, everyone's complexion seemed as flawless as could be expected, and Jennings breathed again.

At two-thirty, two taxis turned into the school drive, and the Bracebridge team arrived, accompanied by an apologetic Mr Parkinson.

"I'm most terribly sorry for that stupid mistake about the quarantine," he said, as Mr Carter greeted him. "It must have put you to considerable inconvenience."

"That's quite all right," Mr Carter assured him. "It didn't cause us any trouble, did it, Wilkins?" He turned to his colleague for confirmation.

"Eh? Oh, no, no, no; not at all; not at all," Mr Wilkins replied hastily, avoiding Mr Carter's eye.

The home team was already on the pitch, resplendent in quartered shirts of magenta and white. In honour of the occasion, Jennings had washed the back of his knees as well as the front, and had obtained some new white laces which he had twisted under and over and round his boots in a cat's cradle of complex design. He then tied two knots on top of the bow for safety, and a third one for luck. The youngest member of the team was ready for the fray!

As soon as the visitors had changed, they streamed out on to the field and Mr Carter, in shorts and blazer, blew his whistle and the game began.

It was soon obvious that the teams were evenly matched, but to start with both sides were keyed up, with their nerves on edge and sharpened by the importance of the occasion. As a result, the standard of play suffered, for an excited atmosphere breeds dashing and wasteful energy rather than careful and scientific play. During the first ten minutes both goals were bombarded with shots, some lucky, some wildly impossible. Gradually, however, their nerves were steadied and their play improved; tactics and skill replaced brute force and ignorance. In fifteen minutes, they had settled down to concentrate on control of the ball, fleetness of foot, and combination of movement.

The teams played in dogged silence, while the spectators on the touch-line shouted encouragement.

"Linbury!" they yelled, in rolling waves of sound, and held on to the last note of their cry until their breath gave out. "Linbury! Play up, Linbury!"

Loudest of all the school supporters was Mr Wilkins. It was as though he kept an amplifier in his throat for these important occasions, and as he swept up and down the touch-line, his thunderous encouragement surged out across the pitch so that the players had difficulty in hearing the referee's whistle. In contrast to this, Bracebridge had only the thin and reedy tones of Mr Parkinson to urge them on, and his voice was as the soft sighing of the west wind compared with Mr Wilkins' stentorian north-easterly gale. The only other supporter for Bracebridge was their linesman who, owing to his role, should really have been impartial, but he was an opportunist, and he carefully waited for the lulls between the shouts for Linbury to squeak, "Play up, Bracebridge!" at the top of his voice.

The play swept from one goal mouth to the other. Now, the Bracebridge forwards had the ball and were attacking strongly. A long, low, swerving shot came in from the left wing and Parslow in goal for Linbury, dived to make a brilliant save. The school clapped and cheered and smacked each other on the back, and Mr Wilkins switched on his loud-hailer at full volume.

"Good save," he boomed. "Jolly well done!"

The ball was cleared and away went the Linbury forwards, Temple, at outside-left, streaking down the field with the ball at his toes. A moment later he, too, had made a long, low, swerving shot and it was the Bracebridge goalkeeper's turn to dive and gather the ball safely to his chest before kicking it clear. Linbury clapped the goalkeeper dutifully while their faces registered disappointment, and Mr Wilkins reduced the volume-control to halfway for his congratulations to the opposing custodian.

The Headmaster, perched precariously on his shooting-stick, looked down the line of spectators to make sure that none had committed the ungentlemanly fault of failing to applaud his opponents.

All through the first half the battle raged evenly and neither side scored. Jennings was playing a hard game, but he knew that he was not playing his best. As it was his first match and he was so much younger than the rest of the side, his sense of nervousness would not wear off. Desperately he sought to make up in dynamic energy what he felt was lacking in cool control.

His first chance came in the second half – and he missed it! Linbury were attacking, and a pass came to him from the left wing. The goalkeeper was out of position and Jennings, with the ball coming straight towards him, was unmarked, less than ten yards from the goal. Even Darbishire could not have missed such an easy shot, and had Jennings been content to direct the ball gently into the net, he would have scored. But the sight of the open goal filled him with a desire to drive the ball with irresistible, net-severing force. He drew back his right foot and swung it forward with all his might – and missed the ball completely! Johnson was just behind him, cool-headed and capable, and avoiding the floundering Jennings, he trapped the ball dead and casually propelled it into the net.

The whistle blew: one-nil.

The crowd on the touch-line went wild with delight while Mr Wilkins, as excited as the youngest of them, shouted, "Goal! Jolly good shot," with such volume that Mr Parkinson, who was standing nearby, decided to watch the rest of the match from the other side of the pitch. He departed, gently massaging his ear to relieve the air-pressure on his eardrum.

Jennings walked up the field feeling very small. It was satisfying to be one goal up, but it was maddening that he, who could have scored so easily, should have thrown away his chance and left the capable Johnson to put the damage right. He tried hard to make up for his lapse and for the next few minutes he played an inspired game.

"Well, I'm doing all right now, anyway," he told himself, and then he proceeded to make his second unforgivable blunder. The Bracebridge forwards were pressing hard now, eager to level the score, and Jennings dropped back to his own penalty area.

"Get up the field," Johnson told him. "You're miles out of position."

Jennings took no notice; he would show them how well he could save a desperate situation, and no one could blame him for being slightly out of his place if he stopped the other side from scoring. He was standing by the side of the goalkeeper when, the Bracebridge centre-half kicked the ball towards the goal. It was never meant to be a shot, and it was not even a good pass, for the ball bounced slowly towards the goalkeeper, and Parslow would have had no difficulty in catching it waist high, and clearing to the wing. He was already cupping his arms to take the ball when Jennings leaped in front of him and attempted a prodigious clearance kick. He was not quite quick enough, however, for instead of taking the ball fairly on his instep, it glanced off the side of his boot and was deflected in a wide parabolic curve into the corner of the net.

The whistle blew: one all.

The groan that rose to the lips of the spectators was silenced by the Headmaster's reproving stare, and, as in duty bound, a tepid clapping of gloved hands was just audible above the delighted squeaks of the Bracebridge linesman.

"Why do we have to clap when we're sorry, sir?" Atkinson asked Mr Wilkins.

"You're applauding your opponents' good play," was the reply.

"But it wasn't good play, sir. Their chap didn't even mean to shoot, did he, sir? It was Jennings who scored, wasn't it, sir?"

"Yes, I suppose it was, really."

"Well, why do we have to clap then, sir?"

"Because… Oh, watch the game," said Mr Wilkins.

Jennings had never felt so unhappy in his life. It was an accident certainly, but a stupid, clumsy sort of accident that would never have happened if he had kept his place and not tried to interfere. Nobody said anything, but their silence was so eloquent that he squirmed with embarrassment as he took his place for the restart of the game. Both sides were playing grimly now; there were only a few minutes to go and the level score urged them to play as though their lives depended on it.

On the touch-line, Darbishire, with notebook in hand, was wondering what to write next. As self-appointed sports reporter, he wanted to give his friend a good press notice, but it was straining the bonds of friendship to have to lavish praise on one who was so obviously responsible for this disaster. He consulted Atkinson and showed him what he had written:

"On the last Saturday of term," Atkinson read, *"a massive crowd of indivigils gathered on the touch-line to witness a gargantuan struggle when we played Bracebridge School in the Royal and Ancient sport of Kings as it is called known as Assosiasion football better known as soccer. They won the toss and chose to play down the inkline although it is not much of a one and you can hardly call it a slope."*

"It's all right up to there," said the press correspondent, "but in the next para. I call Jennings the doughty pivot of the team. Here, look, just after this bit about the ball being literally glued to his flashing feet."

"What's a doughty pivot?" demanded Atkinson.

"I'm not sure," Darbishire replied; "but I got it out of a newspaper, so it's bound to be a pretty stylish way of saying he's spivish rare, and now he's gone and made that frantic bish and scored a goal against us."

"Well, why not leave out all that about the glue on his feet and say that Jennings would have been a pivot if he hadn't made a bish. Benedick's looking at his watch, it must be nearly time."

"Yes, I suppose I... Gosh, what's happening?" Darbishire looked up as the cheers of the spectators rose to a full-throated roar, for in the last minute of the game, Jennings had found his form. Intercepting an opponent's pass, he was off down the field in a flash, dribbling the ball so brilliantly that Darbishire's reference to his flashing feet seemed almost credible. He swerved right and left through the Bracebridge forward line and left the attacking half-backs standing helpless and defeated. The Linbury forwards sprinted down the field in his wake, but they had been hanging back, and Jennings was now a good twenty yards ahead of his colleagues. With a deft flick, he pushed the ball round the Bracebridge full-back and was away again with only the goalkeeper to beat. For a moment the goalkeeper hesitated, started to rush out, changed his mind and retreated between the posts.

Jennings bore down upon him, every line of his body expressing confident determination. He could not fail now. In the fifty-ninth minute of the eleventh hour his chance had come; alone he had swept through the ranks of the opponents and now victory was in sight. One sure, swift shot and he would have made a glorious atonement for his disastrous mistake.

The touch-line seethed with hysterical excitement, but Jennings was oblivious to everything except the ball at his feet, and the agitated goalkeeper ahead. He steadied himself, and drew back his foot for the shot of a lifetime. He could not miss!

He could!

The goal was seven feet high by twenty-one feet wide; the goalkeeper was four and a half feet high and one foot wide. It was the deepest of tragedies that, with nearly one hundred and fifty square feet of goal-mouth yawning like a cavern before him, Jennings had to direct his shot straight at the diminutive figure hopping nervously in the middle of the goal. The goalkeeper cannot be said to have saved the shot, for he was too agitated to be capable of skilful movement, but his presence on the goal-line was sufficient. The ball hit him fairly on the right knee and soared upwards and over the bar.

Jennings did not hear the disappointed groans of the spectators; he stood stock-still, unable to believe his eyes, but the damage was done, and the whistle had sounded for a corner kick. Why, oh, why, did he have to go and throw away the chance of a lifetime? he asked himself, and after that inspired run down the field too! He could have kicked himself. Now, of course, there would be no time to make good the damage, for Mr Carter was looking at his watch and would blow the final whistle immediately after the corner kick had been taken. There was nothing more to be done; he had had every chance to justify his place in the team, and he had failed.

A despairing silence gripped the spectators as Nuttall, on the right wing, prepared to take the corner kick.

Darbishire was busy with his notebook; he had been trying to decide whether Jennings could still be described as a doughty pivot; that last run down the field would certainly have qualified him for the highest honours, but for that final, fatal bish. He compromised by altering the description to "doubtful," pivot, as it had a similar sort of sound without being too lavish in its praise. Then he looked up to watch the last kick being taken. He caught sight of Jennings, and his heart was wrung by his friend's expression of woe. Unmindful of the fact that one does not cheer when the ball is out of play, he suddenly broke the deathly silence by shouting:

"Never mind, Jennings. Better luck next time!"

Nuttall was just running up to take the kick when Darbishire shouted, and, at the sound of his name, Jennings turned his head for a split second towards the spectators on the left touch-line. Thus it was that he did not see the ball hurtling towards his head until it was too late. Out of the corner of his eye, he saw an object about to hit him and, without stopping to think, he jumped to avoid it. His instinct, however, betrayed him, and instead of flinching away from the missile, he jumped right into the trajectory of its flight. With a slight thud, the ball hit him squarely in the middle of his forehead and knocked him off his feet.

He lay on the ground for a moment with his eyes shut, while he recovered from the shock. Thus he did not see the Bracebridge goalkeeper picking the ball from the back of the net; he did not hear Mr Carter blow his whistle to indicate a goal, and immediately afterwards, blow a long, final blast as a signal that the game was over; he was unconscious of the stampede of hysterical delight which swept along the touch-line, as sixty-eight pairs of gum boots executed an ungainly war-dance, while an equal number of vocal chords vied with one another in building up a roaring cataract of cheers.

The first thing Jennings knew was that the entire First Eleven were helping him to his feet and patting him on the back.

"Jolly well done, Jennings," said Nuttall, pounding him heavily between the shoulder blades. "A rare priority smasher!"

"Rather," echoed Temple. "Hefty skilful! Just like a

professional!"

Jennings blinked uncertainly at the ring of smiling faces around him. What on earth were they feeling so pleased about?

"Finest header I've ever seen," said Brown major. "The way you leaped at it and then, wham! – right into the top corner of the net."

"And the force of it, too!" added Johnson. "You must have put all your weight behind it or you wouldn't have gone down flat like that, after you'd whammed it in."

It took Jennings a few seconds to grasp the significance of these remarks. So they had won the match after all, and it was all due to his alleged header in the final second! Well, it was very gratifying, of course, to be acclaimed as the hero of the hour, but what would they say if they knew that his wonder goal was the accidental result of the most frightful bish in the history of soccer?

"Well," he said hesitantly, "it's jolly super of you chaps to be so decent about it, but..." The temptation to bask in unearned glory was strong, but virtuously he decided to tell the truth. "As a matter of fact, the whole thing was just a fluke."

Cries of protest greeted this statement.

"Go and boil yourself," they said affectionately. "You can't fool us like that."

It was all very well to be modest and self-effacing, but Jennings was surely entitled to take the credit for his spectacular shot.

"It was a goal in a thousand," said Temple, admiringly.

"Rats!" said Jennings.

"Well, a goal in a hundred, then."

"Rot!" said Jennings.

"Well, anyway, it was a goal," Temple amended.

"Oh, well," said Jennings. If they wouldn't believe it was

an accident, what more could he say?

Happily, the team escorted their visitors off the pitch.

"There's one thing about old Jennings," Brown major said to Johnson, as he splashed in the   knee-bath some ten minutes later. "He doesn't swank as much as he used to. The way he   back-pedalled about that super header of his; anyone who didn't know, might really think it had been a fluke after all."

"Yes," agreed Johnson, "he certainly knows how to use his head."

13

Mr Carter Makes a Suggestion

Darbishire sat at his desk, busily blacking out squares on a home-made calendar, and as he worked, he sang:

> "*This time next week where shall I be?*
> *Not in this Academy.*"

He licked the worn stub of pencil and bent to his task with far more concentration than he was accustomed to display in class.

> "*We're tired of maths and we're tired of French,*
> *Leaving Latin will be no wrench,*
> *No more of Wilkie's super bates,*
> *When once I'm out of these prison gates,*"

he warbled.

"What are you doing, Darbi?" Jennings asked, strolling about the room with the restless curiosity that the last day of term always brings with it.

"I'm just doing my mammoth how-many-more-to-the-end-of-term calendar," replied the vocalist, ceasing the song abruptly.

Jennings came over to have a look.

"H'm, it's a bit complicated," he remarked, looking, without comprehension, at the maze of squares and figures.

"Yes, but it's superer than the ordinary sort," Darbishire replied proudly. "All the other chaps just have so many more days to the end of term, and just cross out a square every day, but mine's got meals and hours and lessons and things, too. Look, I started it last week and this is how much more there is to go."

Jennings cast his eye over the work of reference.

"Famous Mammoth How-Many-More-To-The-End-Of-Term
Calendar
by
C E J Darbishire, OCC."

"What's OCC?" he inquired.

"Official Calendar Compiler," replied the author with pride.

Beneath these credentials was written:

"No. of days more.   7, 6, 5, 4, 3, 2, 1, 0.
  No. of hours more.   *See page 2. Not enough*
room here.
  No. of Latin lessons.   5, 4, 3, 2, 1, 0.
  No. of times for suet pud.   3, 2, 1, 0.
  No. of times for clean sox. 2, 1, 0."

Jennings raised an objection.

"s-o-x doesn't spell socks."

"Well, what does it spell?" demanded Darbishire, logically.

"s-o-x spells – well, of course it does, really," Jennings conceded.

"There you are, then," replied the OCC. "I know how to

spell socks as well as anyone, but that's another of my inventions. Shorthand, you see; it saves wearing your wrist out when everyone knows what you mean anyway."

Over the page, the number of hours remaining filled seventeen lines. Starting at the imposing total of one hundred and sixty-eight, the figures had been crossed out until only twenty-one remained.

"It's a bit of a hairy fag, of course, crossing out the hours," Darbishire explained, " 'cos sometimes when it's time to cross one off, you're doing something else, but it's wizard to come downstairs in the morning and swoosh off about ten all in one go."

Jennings was impressed. His own calendar consisted of a drawing of a wall with ten green bottles hanging from it. Every day he had rubbed out one bottle and had drawn what was meant to represent the mounting débris of broken glass at the bottom of the wall. Darbishire had obviously tackled his task more thoroughly. Perhaps next term, Jennings decided, he would go one better and keep a tally of the passing time in minutes. He took pencil and paper to work out the details, and only abandoned his scheme when he discovered that there were some ten thousand minutes in a week, and it would be more than a full-time job trying to keep the record up to date.

The school was in the grip of that mounting excitement which always accompanies the last days of term. tuck-boxes had been packed days before it was necessary; and desks were tidied, untidied and re-tidied daily, in order to nourish the feeling of impending departure which these preparations always brought with them. Completely useless articles which were discovered in the murkier recesses of tuck-boxes and lockers were bartered freely, and the announcement, "Quis for a piece of junk!" would be answered by a deafening, "Ego!" which shattered the fast-crumbling nerves of the less placid members of the staff.

With an artistic flourish, Darbishire completed the current entries on his mammoth calendar.

"What shall we do now?" he demanded.

"Let's go and pack our tuck-boxes again," Jennings suggested.

"But I've only just done mine," said Darbishire.

"Never mind," Jennings replied. "It's our last chance, 'cos they'll be taking them to the station this afternoon. Oh, wiz! I can hardly believe we're going home tomorrow. Come on, let's be bombers."

With outstretched arms, they wheeled and circled round the room.

"Eee-ow-ow... Eee-ow-ow – !" The bombers banked steeply to get through the door, and only the pilots' skill and their patent retractable wingtips saved the planes from serious damage.

"Eee-ow-ow... Eee-ow-ow – ! Dacka-dacka-dacka-dacka!"

The tail gunner of "J for Jennings" squeezed the trigger for a five-second burst that went through the passage window and shot up a tradesman's van which was just turning into the drive. Unaware that he had been liquidated, the vanman drove steadily on – a spirit driver in a phantom chariot.

The pilots flew towards the tuck-box room by dead reckoning, alert to notice every new sign that portended the passing of the term. Timetables, notices and regulations, had all been taken down. The library shelves were full, and the boot-lockers were empty. Masters clutching files of reports, and lists of travelling arrangements, moved purposefully along corridors, and their expressions were harassed or happy, according to how much of their work still remained to be done.

Old Pyjams, assisted by the gardener, was lowering trunks out of the dormitory windows on the end of a rope. They were watched by an enthralled crowd of boys, filled with the secret hope that the rope might break when someone else's trunk had started its journey. They climbed on the luggage as it was piled up on the quad, and as each trunk appeared on the window-sill, it was greeted by rousing cheers from the watchers below.

"Come up here," called Venables; "it makes a super grand stand!"

Old Pyjams shouted from above: "Come on off of it, some of you," as the trunk lids sagged beneath their load.

"We can't possibly come on off till we've seen our own trunks come down," Jennings reasoned. "Supposing they got left behind?"

At last they were rewarded by seeing their luggage dangling on the end of the rope, and completely satisfied, they set course once more for the tuck-box room.

At the bottom of Darbishire's tuck-box they found a notebook. The covers were slightly smeared with marmalade and chocolate spread, and an occasional date stone dropped from between the clog-eared pages as Darbishire turned them over.

" '*Flixton Slick – Super Sleuth*,' " he announced reverently. "And we never got beyond the first chapter!"

"We can still take it to Mr Carter," said Jennings. "Tell him it's the first instalment of a serial and we'll get chapter two written next term – p'r'aps."

"Yes, but would he put it in the mag.?" mused Darbishire. "He turned down my special sports reporter account of the Bracebridge match."

"He never did!" Jennings exclaimed. "Why, it was jolly good; especially those four pages about me."

"He said the style was too ex – something."

"Exciting?"

"No, execrable, I think. And, anyway, he said thirteen

pages was too long; he made me cut out all those super descriptions and all the atmosphere I'd carefully worked up, and by the time I'd got it short enough for him, all that was left was, '*The First Eleven beat Bracebridge by two goals to one on the last Saturday of term*,' and it didn't seem worth calling it a special report with my signature underneath, just for that!"

"Well, never mind," Jennings consoled him. "If he's turned down your football account, he can't very well refuse Flixton Slick, 'cos that'd probably discourage us, and he keeps on about how we ought to send stuff in to be printed."

"Okay, then," agreed Darbishire, "let's take it up to him when we go to bed, because there's the ping-pong tournament this afternoon, and films this evening."

Mr Carter was always busy on the last evening of term. After a hurried cup of tea, he returned to his room and set to work. The boys' train tickets and travelling arrangements were stacked in a neat pile ready to be given out at breakfast on the following morning. His empty cash box witnessed that the school bank had satisfied its last customer. So far so good. He took up a folder from his desk containing a sheaf of reports; he would finish these first, and then begin the more exacting task of editing the manuscripts intended for the school magazine.

For forty minutes he concentrated on the reports and then, with a sigh of relief, he noticed that only one more remained to be done. When he saw that the sheet was headed "J C T Jennings" he was glad that he had left it till the last, for he was not sure how to express his opinion. On the one hand, Jennings was keen, alert, willing, truthful, polite and bubbling over with high-spirited enthusiasm for everything that was going on about him; yet, when Mr Carter cast his mind back over the more hair-raising events of the term, he could not help thinking how these virtuous qualities belonged to one who repeatedly dropped metaphorical spanners into the smooth-running machine of school life. Attached to the report was a note from the Headmaster to the effect that Mr Jennings still seemed uncertain whether his son was settling down as he should, and would Mr Carter make some suitable comment on this in his house master's report.

He was considering what to write when he heard furtive whispers outside the door.

"Bags you knock, Darbishire," said the first whisperer.

"No, bags you; it's mostly my story, so I don't like to seem too eager," he heard the second voice reply.

"Well, I'll just do a soft buff then, in case he's busy and doesn't want to be disturbed."

Mr Carter called, "Come in," quickly, to forestall the thunderous onslaught on the door panels that he knew would follow this announcement. "I'm terribly busy," he said.

"Shall we hoof off, then, sir?"

"Shall you what?"

"Oh, sorry, sir. I mean, shall we take our departure, sir?"

"You'd better wait outside for a moment; I'm writing reports."

"Have you done mine yet, sir?" Jennings asked. "Hope you're going to give me a super decent one, sir. What are you going to say about my football, sir?"

"Yes, sir," Darbishire put in. "You ought to say something spivish smashing after that goal he headed on Saturday, sir."

"I think the less said about that goal the better," said Mr Carter, meaningly.

Jennings looked uncomfortable.

"Did you know it was a fluke, then, sir?" he asked.

"I'm afraid I did," Mr Carter replied. "I was standing a lot nearer to you than the spectators were, and in my experience the best goals are never headed with the eyes tightly shut."

Jennings looked more uncomfortable.

"Well, I did tell them it was a fluke, sir, but they wouldn't believe me; and we've got something here for the magazine we want to show you, sir," he said, quickly changing the subject.

"Well, if you like to wait on the landing while I finish this report, I'll see you in a few minutes."

"Yes, sir." They retired, closing the door behind them.

Mr Carter found it impossible to concentrate with Jennings and Darbishire standing outside in the corridor. The door was by no means soundproof, and every low-toned syllable was clearly audible. He tried vainly to sum up Jennings' character in a few well-chosen words as the Headmaster had requested, but all the time he found himself becoming more and more engrossed in the conversation that was going on, in reverberating whispers, outside his door.

"It'd be the wizardest of prangs," Jennings was saying, " 'cos if we've got something to eat that's really cooked, we can pretend our carriage is a dining-car, and we shall be ever so hungry, 'cos we shan't have had any breakfast if we put them in our pockets to eat on the school train."

"But s'posing they're not hard-boiled?" the listener heard Darbishire object. "It's all very well to say let's put them in our pockets for a feast, but if they smash and run all over the linings, we shall be almost dead with hunger by the time the train gets there, because of not eating them at breakfast time."

"Don't be such a bazooka," Jennings replied. "We've had eggs for breakfast every Friday this term, haven't we? And have you ever known them to be anything but hard?"

"Well, no, I haven't," Darbishire was forced to admit.

"Well, then, that proves it. You know what they're like in school kitchens; they can't be bothered to boil them for long enough to make them really nice and soft."

Mr Carter returned to his report. "*He enters very fully into all out-of-school activities, and takes a lively interest in the corporate life of the school*," he wrote.

"Talk quietly, or else he'll hear us," Jennings went on, and Mr Carter could imagine the finger pointed towards his door.

"Now, there'll be eight chaps in our carriage, and if we all put our eggs in our pockets and eat them when we get on the train, we can chuck the empty shells at the chaps farther down the train when they put their heads out of the windows. Wizard prang!"

Thumps in the corridor indicated that an informal dance was being held to celebrate this idea.

Mr Carter turned to the report again, and wrote: "*He has a vivid imagination and definite qualities of leadership, but these traits must be carefully guided into the right channels.*" And he made a mental note to see that all the breakfast eggs were consumed on the premises.

"Okay, then, we'll do that," said Darbishire, as the dance ended. "It'll be super, won't it?"

"Witch prang!" exclaimed Jennings.

"What do you mean, which prang? There is only one.'

"No, I don't mean which prang, I mean Witch Prang. W-I-T-C-H. You know, black cats, and flying on broomsticks."

"Who's flying on broomsticks?" Darbishire wanted to know.

"Witches do."

"Well, what if they do? What about it?"

"Nothing," explained Jennings, with some impatience. "Only when you agreed to my wheeze, I just said Witch Prang."

"Why?"

"It's the feminine of Wizard Prang. Witch Prang is Wizard Prang's wife."

"How d'you know?"

Mr Carter felt that the conversation was getting beyond him.

"I made up a story about them in bed the other night," he heard Jennings say. "I shall probably ask Benedick to put it in the mag. when it's done, only he might turn it down, 'cos there aren't many murders and things in it."

Mr Carter raised despairing eyes to the heavens.

"You see, the neighbours don't know they can work spells," Jennings went on, "and they just think they're Mr and Mrs W Prang of 'Elm Villa,' and they've got a son called Goblin Prang, Esq., who works in a post office... Oh, yes, and Mrs Witch Prang doesn't have a broomstick, she flies in a super autogyro, and instead of a magic cauldron she's got a thermostic-controlled electric dishwasher and..."

In despair, Mr Carter stopped working and called them in.

"Now, then," he said. "What is it you want to see me about?"

Shyly, Darbishire produced his masterpiece.

"This is just the first instalment of a little thing we dashed off for the magazine, sir," he said.

Mr Carter glanced through the pages of "*Flixton Slick – Super Sleuth.*" He sighed. It seemed a poor reward for a term spent in teaching them to write English. Why couldn't they write something that didn't depend upon impossible hairbreadth escapes? Why this untidy pile of corpses that littered every other page?

"I wish you wouldn't model your style on 'blood and thunders,' " he said. "I don't encourage you to read them."

"Well, sir, you do sometimes," said Darbishire; "because you told us to read *Treasure Island*, and my father says Stevenson wrote it as weekly instalments for a penny dreadful, so if you print Flixton Slick in the mag. in little bits, it might turn out to be a classic just like *Treasure Island* did."

"Yes," said Mr Carter; "but your style isn't as good as Robert Louis Stevenson's."

"Oh, but, sir, we went to an awful lot of trouble and looked up all the best authors, sir." Darbishire took up the notebook and scanned the pages in search of an example. "Look at this bit, sir, you can't say this isn't classical."

Mr Carter read:

"Flixton Slick was bound hand and foot and was wondering how to get free when he saw that the Silent Shadow had accidentally left a dagger on the table. That gave him an idea for he had been highly educated and was on nodding terms with the Bard. 'Ha!' he said. 'Is this a dagger that I see before me the handle toward my hand. Come let me clutch thee.' He stretched forward but he could not quite reach it. 'Oh dash it,' he exclaimed. 'I have thee not and yet I see thee still. If only I could get thee I could get free and then I could photograph the fingerprints before the filthy witness washes his hands.'"

Mr Carter laid down the book.

"You see what I mean, sir?" said Darbishire. "I borrowed quite a lot of that from *Macbeth*, and you can't say Shakespeare isn't good style, can you, sir?"

Mr Carter groaned. "I'm sorry," he said; "but it's just too dreadful; I can't possibly put this sort of stuff in the magazine."

He rose from his desk and paced the room, while Jennings and Darbishire watched him reproachfully. They felt he ought to be looking pleased at having such gifted contributors to assist him to fill up his columns, but instead of that his expression conveyed that he, too, like Macbeth and Flixton Slick, was suffering from a surfeit of daggers of the mind. Mr Carter was conscious of their unspoken reproach: Darbishire gazed beadily at him through his spectacles, and Jennings stood on one leg and massaged his right calf with his left foot. Their attitude plainly said that Mr Carter was falling painfully short of the qualities demanded of a literary talent spotter.

Finally Mr Carter spoke.

"Have you ever met any detectives or criminals, socially?"

"No, sir," answered Jennings, somewhat surprised.

"Then you can't expect anything you write about them to be convincing. If you're going to write a story for the magazine, choose a subject that you really know something about."

Jennings and Darbishire looked at each other, and their glances clearly indicated what they thought of Mr Carter's suggestion.

"What could we write about then, sir?" Jennings asked.

Mr Carter considered.

"Well, think of all that's happened since you came here, and try describing your first term at school."

"Oh, sir, that'd be silly," objected Jennings. "Nothing ever happens at school; no murders; no crooks; never anything exciting; and everybody here is so ordinary. We never get a chance to do anything worth writing about."

"Oh, I don't know," replied Mr Carter. "You think it over. You might call it – er – something like, *'Jennings Goes to School.'*"

Jennings was sceptical; it was all very well for grown-ups to make absurd and impossible suggestions. He'd like to see them do it.

"Well, sir," he said at length, and his tone was most polite, "don't think I'm trying to be critical, sir, but if you think it's such a good idea, why don't you do it yourself?"

"I might," Mr Carter replied unexpectedly. "It's certainly

an idea."

Disappointed, the two authors took their leave. Outside in the corridor, where they mistakenly supposed that they were out of earshot, Jennings and Darbishire expressed their views on Mr Carter's shortcomings as a literary critic.

"I think Benedick's crackers," said Darbishire.

"He's more than that," said Jennings, "he's superscrewy squared. Why, I bet you a million pounds nobody in their senses would ever want to read stories about chaps like us!"

On the other side of the door Mr Carter smiled as he filled his pipe.

"Wouldn't they?" he murmured to himself. "I'm not so sure."

Anthony Buckeridge

Jennings and Darbishire

Prehistoric clodpoll!

'What did you want to go and make a frantic bish like that for? Rule number nine million and forty-seven: Any boy beetling into class with twelve slippery raw fish shall hereby be liable to be detained during Mr Wilkins' pleasure.'

Jennings turns journalist when he receives a printing kit for his birthday, and dubs himself Editor of the *Form Three Times*. Enlisting faithful Darbi as his assistant hack, Jennings sets off to the cove, where a French fishing vessel is moored, for their first story. But when their dreadful French ends in the unwelcome gift of a parcel of raw fish, the worst place they could hide it is in Mr Wilkins' chimney!

Frantic hoo-hah!

Teething troubles fail to deter the tenacious Jennings, and his next scoop involves digging into Mr Wilkins' past – what will he uncover this time?

Super-wacko wheeze!

ANTHONY BUCKERIDGE

JENNINGS FOLLOWS A CLUE

Fossilized fish-hooks!

'We must have a headquarters, where we can meet and work out clues and things. We might even put up a notice so that chaps will know where to come when they want mysteries solved. Something like *Linbury Court Detective Agency – Chief Investigator, J C T Jennings…*'

When Jennings is inspired to take up a career as a detective, with faithful Darbishire as his assistant, trouble is bound to be just around the corner. Their first mission – to recover a 'stolen' sports cup – is the first of several bungled attempts to imitate super sleuth Sherlock Holmes.

Frightful bish!

But the detective duo face their most perilous adventure yet when they make a nocturnal visit to the sanatorium and discover that they are not alone. An intruder is at large, but a missing coat button is Jennings' only clue.

Crystallised cheesecakes!

Anthony Buckeridge

Jennings' Little Hut

Supersonic hoo-hah!

Jennings and Darbishire watched with mounting horror. Earthquakes and landslides seemed to be happening before their eyes. The little hut was heaving like a thing possessed. 'Oh, fish-hooks!' breathed Jennings in dismay. 'He's smashing up the place like a bulldozer!'

The woodland at Linbury Court becomes squatters' territory when Jennings comes up with the idea of building huts out of reeds and branches. Jennings and Darbishire are thrilled with their construction, which even includes a patented prefabricated ventilating shaft, a special irrigation drainage canal and a pontoon suspension bridge!

Gruesome hornswoggler!

But things can only go horribly wrong for Jennings when he is put in charge of Elmer, the treasured goldfish, and even worse when the Headmaster pays the squatters a visit. And if Jennings thinks that a game of cricket will be far less trouble, he's going to be knocked for six!

Rotten chizzler!